Honest Mistake

LISA SUZANNE

HONEST MISTAKE
VEGAS ACES: THE WIDE RECEIVER
BOOK THREE
© 2022 Lisa Suzanne

All rights reserved. In accordance with the US Copyright Act of 1976, the scanning, uploading, and sharing of any part of this book without the permission of the publisher or author constitute unlawful piracy and theft of the author's intellectual property. No part of this book may be reproduced or transmitted in any form or by any means, electronic or mechanical, including photocopying, recording, or by any information storage and retrieval system without the written permission of the author, except where permitted by law and except for excerpts used in reviews. If you would like to use any words from this book other than for review purposes, prior written permission must be obtained from the publisher.

Published in the United States of America by Books by LS, LLC.

ISBN: 9798352792438

This book is a work of fiction. Any similarities to real people, living or dead, is purely coincidental. All characters and events in this work are figments of the author's imagination.

BOOKS BY LISA SUZANNE

VEGAS ACES
Home Game (Book One)
Long Game (Book Two)
Fair Game (Book Three)
Waiting Game (Book Four)
End Game (Book Five)

VEGAS ACES: THE QUARTERBACK
Traded (Book One)
Tackled (Book Two)
Timeout (Book Three)
Turnover (Book Four)
Touchdown (Book Five)

VEGAS ACES: THE TIGHT END
Tight Spot (Book One)
Tight Hold (Book Two)
Tight Fit (Book Three)
Tight Laced (Book Four)
Tight End (Book Five)

A LITTLE LIKE DESTINY SERIES
A Little Like Destiny (Book One)
Only Ever You (Book Two)
Clean Break (Book Three)

Visit Lisa on Amazon for more titles

DEDICATION

For my three favorite people.

CHAPTER 1

Tristan

"I'm pregnant."

The high I've been riding after catching evidence on Savannah and serving her with the final papers seems to deflate at her words.

I knew she was holding onto something…but I wasn't expecting her to tell me *that*.

All the blood seems to drain from my face, and I feel a little dizzy at the rush.

"You're…" I trail off.

"Pregnant," she says again.

We've spent nearly every day together since we arrived back in town on the same day well over a month ago.

How could she be pregnant?

Okay, fine. I know *how*.

Maybe the better question is *how did she keep it from me*? Or even better…how did I not realize it?

And maybe most importantly…does she have a relationship with the father?

I start to form one of those questions on my tongue, but I find it a little too twisted to actually speak coherently right now.

"But how—I mean when, or who…" I shake my head as I try to reconcile her words with everything that's happened over the last month and a half.

We haven't toasted with alcohol since we've been back, but maybe she's not a big drinker.

I think back to the few times we drank together when we were kids. I held her hair when she puked, climbed in her window and slept on the floor beside her to make sure she was okay, helped come up with alibis so she'd never have to admit to her strict parents what we were really up to. She vowed to never drink again more than once. Maybe she kept true to that promise, though I somehow doubt it.

She doesn't *look* pregnant. But it's winter, and it's damn cold here in Fallon Ridge. She's been bundled up in sweatshirts, and maybe she's not showing yet.

Or maybe she is. Hard to tell. She has a glow emanating from her, but I figured it was the glow of her beauty, not of pregnancy.

And every time I've tried to get *physically* close to her, she's backed away, citing all the things I don't know as her excuse. I guess what I didn't know is that she's growing a baby.

I clear my throat as I try to come to terms with this news. "How far along are you?"

She draws in a breath. "Six months."

"Six months?" I practically yell.

How the fuck is she six months along and I'm just finding out about it now? I glance down at her stomach. Surely she's showing at this stage of her pregnancy, but she's in yet another bulky sweatshirt that hides away what's happening inside her body.

How could I have been so oblivious?

She nods, and the fear in her eyes is evident. "I was so scared to tell you," she whispers. "I was so afraid we'd get close, or we'd cross the line to get back where we were before, but then you'd find out and it would scare you off. It's why I've tried keeping my distance. It's why I—"

"Used my marriage as an excuse not to get close to me," I murmur, finishing her sentence for her.

Anger vibrates in my chest as I get a look at this new woman standing in front of me.

She's not my girl. She's not the one I used to know.

And yet…I've fallen in love with who she is now despite the huge secret she's been keeping. I don't know how I could fall for someone I feel like I hardly know, but I know what I feel. She's different than she was before, but so am I.

I'm not sure what that means. I'm not sure where we go from here.

"That's not true," she says, and her voice cracks with emotion as a tear slips onto her cheek. "I can't get involved with someone who took vows with someone else. Especially not when the father…the father…" She chokes on her words, the tears coming faster now.

"Who's the father?" I whisper, even though I already know the answer.

"Cam. The doctor from the office who was married. The one who won an award for his family values. The one who told me to *take care of it* when I told him I was pregnant."

"To *take care of it*? What does that even mean?" I ask, the anger vibrating harder in my chest but for a different reason now.

She shakes her head. "I think it meant something different to him than it did to me. I am going to take care of it," she says, air quoting the words he used. "For the rest of her life."

"Her?" I say softly. "You're having a girl?"

She nods as she presses her lips together, and more tears fall from her eyes. "He doesn't want anything to do with her. With me. With us. When he won that award and promised some of the grant money to Paul, my old boss…I couldn't get in the way of that. I couldn't make some public scandal even though the world deserves to know what a trash human he is."

I have the sudden urge to hold her. I don't know what this means—for her, for us, for everything…but the woman I love is standing before me, hurting and scared as she cries for everything she's been through, and my job is to provide her comfort in this time of need.

I close the gap between us and take her in my arms. She slides her arms around my waist and rests her head on my chest as I clutch her tightly to me, and for the first time, I feel the bump of her belly pressing into me.

This is the first time I've held her in my arms. The first time we've been this close.

The first time she's let down her guard enough to let me touch her like this.

I breathe her in, the soft scent of her sweet jasmine telling me this is the same woman I've loved over half my life despite the changes. She's been through a lot over the last six months, and she's been doing it largely alone.

I'm angry, sure. I'm hurt she didn't think she could tell me. I'm confused about what happens next—if anything at all, or if the road of hope for us ends here.

But a tiny glimmer locked away deep in my heart has me wondering whether this could be the start of everything I've ever wanted…with the right woman this time.

CHAPTER 2

Tessa

I could stand here in his arms forever, but I'm still bracing myself for his reaction.

I realize in this moment that we're in the same place we were seven years ago. It's like we're picking up where we left off. We were in love, and I was pregnant…only I never got the chance to tell him.

And this time, the baby isn't his.

He pulls back, and I gaze up into his eyes. His are cloudy and confused for a beat before he closes them, and he lowers his head and drops his lips to mine.

It starts soft and slow, just like I remember, and then old habits seem to wash over both of us as I clutch onto him and his mouth opens to mine. It moves from slow and tender into hot and urgent, our tongues battering together with total abandon. He's about to gain his freedom back, and I'm about to lose mine in a lot of ways, and even though it's confusing and scary and there's still so much unknown between us…somehow this kiss feels like the exact thing I need in this moment.

It's telling me that while he might be angry or confused or scared, too, he's not giving up on me. On *us*.

And that's everything I was terrified about leading up to finally making my confession. He didn't ask me to leave. He didn't run.

Instead, he pulled me into his arms, and now he's kissing me like he's a starved man who needs my mouth for his nourishment. He's worshipping me with his lips as he holds my body to his, and all the feelings that I always felt for him come back with a vengeance. It's stronger now—like even though there are still secrets looming between us, we've experienced other things and people but realize that nobody, *nobody* can hold a candle to what we had together.

The butterflies that used to flap low in my belly are back, and maybe they're flying in a ring around baby girl, because she's suddenly spurred into action.

I don't know how long we stand in his garage kissing, but I do feel baby girl kick as my body is pressed against his. He feels it, too. He slows the kiss, but he doesn't end it. He loosens his grip on me and trails a hand down to my belly, and as he rests it there softly, tenderly, she kicks again.

He pulls back, his cloudy, lust-filled eyes a mirror of my own, but his are filled with surprise. "Was that her?"

I nod, a little smile playing at my lips. "I think she likes you. She's been kicking a lot at night lately, but it's usually when I lie down to go to sleep."

He chuckles, but then he nods down toward his hand. "Is this okay?"

I nod.

"I want to feel it again," he says softly.

We both wait, and she's quiet.

"It's amazing that you have a life growing inside you. That she's growing and moving. Isn't that…" he trails off. "I don't know. Women are just the most incredible, badass creatures that they can do that."

She kicks again at his words, and we both chuckle.

"She's going to be a little badass soccer star," he says. His eyes move back to mine. "I don't know what this means, Tess. I don't know where we go from here. We have a lot to work through, a lot to say to each other…but I'm not running scared. Okay? We'll figure out the next step. Together…if you want me here."

My eyes fill with tears again at his words. "Of course I want you here."

He presses his lips to mine again, and suddenly I don't feel so alone.

But I'm still holding onto a pretty big secret. He didn't run scared after tonight's confession, but how do I tell him about what happened all those years ago? How do I even begin that conversation…and will it just drive a huge wedge between the two of us when we're finally turning a corner?

I don't think he'll run scared. Not after the way he reacted to baby girl.

But I'm still not ready to risk that tonight, not when we're finally on a new road together.

Let's just get through one baby crisis at a time. Then once she's here, and we have our own routine and we've figured out where we stand with one another…maybe that'll be the time to tell him what happened all those years ago.

Or not.

We can't do anything about it, and I still wonder whether it's best left in the past.

He moves toward the bench in the garage and sits. "Do you have it in writing that the doctor is giving up his rights?"

I shake my head. "My mom asked me that, too, but the things he said…he doesn't want anything to do with us. I don't even think he'd sign a paper saying he's giving up rights because that would be admitting it's his and that he does have some legal ties to this baby." I set my hand over my stomach as I sit next to him.

"You're sure?" he asks. "After dealing with Savannah, I guess I've learned a thing or two about how slimy people operate. I just want you to protect yourself." He sets his hand over mine where it rests on my stomach. "And her."

I nod. "Maybe I should. Just to be safe."

"I can have my lawyer send the papers over to the doctor. Nobody ever needs to know anything about it, and we'll have the paperwork to keep him away should he ever change his mind."

"You wouldn't mind?" I ask.

He shakes his head. "I'll do anything to help, Tess."

I nod. "Okay. Tell me what you need and we can send the paperwork over."

He sends a text presumably to his lawyer, and he tosses an arm over the back of the bench. I lean into him as I start daydreaming of a life with Tristan and this baby girl.

Can I really have it all?

Time will tell, but in this moment…it's sure starting to look that way.

CHAPTER 3

Tristan

"She's *pregnant?*" my mom asks over spaghetti and meatballs.

I nod.

"Dang, that Janet can sure keep a secret," she murmurs.

"When is she due?" my dad asks.

"She's six months along." I take a bite of garlic bread. "She was, uh, *dating* a doctor she worked with, and he turned out to be married. Told her he didn't want anything to do with the baby, and I guess he's pretty high-profile and can't afford the scandal."

"She's protecting him?" my dad presses.

"Not exactly. He won some award that came with grant money, and he's sharing some of that money with her old boss. She's protecting *him* and her old place of employment, not the father," I say. "She really loved her job. Said her boss was like a second father to her."

"So she came here to hide out?" my mom correctly guesses.

"It would seem so. And then fate brought me back here at the same time." I glance over at my dad. Did he get sick so fate could push Tessa and me together?

I feel a little nauseated at the thought even though my logical side tells me it's nonsense.

"Fate?" my mom asks. "Wait a minute…you aren't suggesting—"

I cut her off. "Be careful, Mom."

Her brows dip. "You're going to be by her side as her *friend*, right?"

I'm quiet a minute as I process her words and their underlying meaning. What she really means is that I shouldn't get involved with someone who's having somebody else's child. But I'm not *getting involved* with her. I never *stopped* being involved with her.

I don't care that it's someone else's baby. One-half of that baby's genes come from Tessa, and that's all that matters to me.

We can have one of our own next, God willing, and I will love and raise both children in the same way.

I want to be with Tessa. I've *always* wanted to be with Tessa.

I want children, and I want them with her.

Maybe this isn't the way I pictured it when I was a seventeen-year-old in love. My parents will tell me I'm young, that I don't know what I'm doing, that this is the wrong decision.

But being there for her, holding her hand at the doctor's visits, and being that child's father…they're big decisions, sure. I should spend some time thinking about it all.

But my gut tells me this is what's right. This is where I need to be.

Why else would she show up out of the blue at home the same time as me when we've both stayed away so long?

Why else would she show up pregnant and able to give me all the very things I've been craving in my life?

It feels like more than just fate stepping in.

It feels like I was dropped in this place at this time for a reason, and maybe that reason is to give her child the father she deserves.

I don't know if I've ever felt so strongly about anything in my life.

There's just one problem that keeps nagging at the back of my mind.

I just caught my wife cheating on me. I told her I never cheated, and I pressed forward with the divorce. Now I just need to sit back quietly and wait for it to go through.

But that wife of mine?

She'll dig.

If she hasn't already, she will find out I've been spending time with a pregnant woman, and if Tessa and I land in a place where I become a father to her baby publicly, well, Savannah will question whether or not I cheated on her…or worse, she'll dig until she discovers who the father is.

If she doesn't already know.

And that thought is terrifying.

Speaking of my lovely wife, I realize I never really took a good look at the photos I took of the shit she had in that jewelry box.

"I love her," I finally say to answer my mother's question. "I will be there for her in whatever way we agree is the right way for us."

My dad lets out a harrumph of disapproval. "Babies are a lot of work, kiddo. Middle of the night feedings, dirty diapers…it's not a glamorous lifestyle, and it's certainly not the bachelor life you've become accustomed to."

"You may recall that I'm married," I say dryly. "I'm not living the bachelor life."

"Exactly," my mom adds. "And what will it do to your divorce proceedings if you're playing off like this baby is yours?"

I should've guessed my parents would ask the hard questions over dinner when I simply decided to tell them Tessa is pregnant. I should've guessed this is where the conversation would go.

I know they're only pressing because they love me. They want what's best for me. But what if what they think is best for me and what I think is best for me are two completely different paths?

It's my life.

I can listen to their words of wisdom and their advice, and I can take it or leave it.

And if they're sitting here telling me not to stand by the side of the only woman I've ever loved in her time of need…well, it's likely I will choose not to take their advice.

They're the ones who were there at the end of what Tessa and I shared the first time. They were the ones pushing me to focus on something other than the girl who held my heart…the girl who broke my heart. We knew she disappeared, and we knew she wasn't coming back. Her parents made sure we knew that.

Her father had something to do with it. I'm sure of it, and I still intend to get to the bottom of things. But she just told me she's pregnant. She's going through enough emotional upheaval at the moment. We can dig into the past later.

Besides, whatever happened back then…it won't change how I feel about her now. Whatever reason her father had for sending her away couldn't make me love her any differently.

My parents were also the ones pushing me to focus on football when she left so I wouldn't fall into a desperate pit of depression with no way out.

I get that they're worried. I know they're scared history will repeat itself.

But Tessa and I…we're in different places now. We're not dumb kids waiting for our parents to leave so we can find time to fuck.

We're adults with adult problems. I'm married. She's pregnant.

And somehow…I feel like none of that matters. We can figure this out. We can make this work.

I will not listen to people trying to talk me out of it.

I already lost her once. I won't lose her again.

CHAPTER 4

Tessa

"I told my parents," he says softly.

"What did they say?" I tug the blanket up around my stomach. The weather is starting to warm up a little, but the nights are still chilly beside an open window…or maybe the chill I'm feeling comes from the fear that his parents know.

More people are finding out.

It only makes things more real…and it only presents a bigger risk of more people finding out who the real father is.

"A lot of things," he mutters. "My mom was surprised your mom kept it from her."

"She did it at my request. It's not that I was lying to anybody or anything…I just wasn't ready to talk about it." I clear my throat as emotion seems to clog it for a beat. "I'm still not. It's embarrassing that it happened the way it did. And it's like…people know I have *sex*." I whisper the last word.

"There's nothing shameful about that, Tess, despite what your father tried to make you believe." His voice is low as he says the words, but I realize how much my religion was drilled into me from a young age. I started to shed some of those beliefs as I took on my independence in Chicago—as I moved out of my father's restrictive shadow—but knowing what he did in his free time despite what he tried to teach me has really sent my morality meter into total chaos.

Tristan was raised so differently than me. His house was sex positive, where it was a taboo subject in mine. And yet…he's not the one who's having a baby out of wedlock. Just because his family talked about it doesn't mean he sleeps around, and just because mine didn't doesn't mean I acted out of rebellion to get to where I am.

"I know," I mumble as I study my blanket so I don't feel his eyes burning into me…judging me.

"Hey," he says softly. I glance over at him, and his eyes are genuine as they stare at me. Not judgmental.

"What?"

"It's okay. It might not be how you imagined things, but you're not alone. Okay?"

I nod. "Okay."

But that's kind of the thing. Maybe I'm not alone right now, but I *will be*. He's a young, very attractive, successful celebrity. He can have his pick of whoever he wants in the entire world, and somehow I doubt that's the girl next door who's about to become a single mother. He'll need to go back to Vegas at some point, and then what?

He must be able to tell from my single word response that I'm not convinced.

He stands, disappears for a few seconds—presumably to grab his shoes—then opens his window. The very second he stood, I knew what he planned to do, and my hunch is correct. He climbs through his window, and just like old times, he skips the few steps across the yard separating us and opens my window wider. I move off my windowsill, and he climbs into my bedroom.

Now *this*…this feels like old times.

I can't help a breathless laugh as he takes me into his arms. "You're not alone," he repeats. He leans his forehead to mine.

"I know." I hear it in my own voice, so I'm sure he detects it, too. Fear.

"Then what are you scared of?" he whispers.

I pull out of his arms and move toward my bed to sit. "This is nice now, but I'm having a baby, Tristan. A baby that isn't yours, and you're still married to someone else. Even if you're here for me, even if the things I didn't even dare to dream actually come true and somehow we end up back together—which I can't even ask of you given that I'm pregnant with somebody else's child—eventually you'll have to go back to Vegas. You'll have to go back to your life, and you *should* go back to your life. You deserve to. You don't deserve to be tied down to some ex-girlfriend because you feel some sense of responsibility to make up for the past."

He presses his lips together. "Is that what you think this is?"

I shrug and hold up my hands as if to say, *prove me wrong*.

He shakes his head, and I think I sense a little disgust in the action.

"What?" I challenge.

He sighs as he averts his eyes over toward the window. "It's not obligation. It's not responsibility."

"Then what?" I ask, a desperate, pleading quality clouding my voice.

He shakes his head before he turns back toward me. He paces a little as he speaks. "It's love, Tessa Taylor. Pure, plain, and simple. We might've just been teenagers, but we had something special."

He stops pacing and he turns to face me. "Maybe I held you up on some pedestal after you walked out of my life, but I knew it wasn't because of you. I knew there was something else at play, something you didn't tell me, something you *couldn't* tell me, maybe, something I'm not even sure I want you to tell me at this point because it's in the past and I don't think it matters anymore."

My breath catches in my throat as he refers to that time, and a sense of relief falls onto my shoulders at his words. He's giving me permission not to tell him what happened. It feels freeing at the same time it feels…weird.

"You're pregnant, and that baby you're growing deserves to be your focus. We're here now. We found our way back, somehow, some way, and I think it's because it's fate." He sighs as he turns toward the window. "All I've been thinking about over the last few months is how I want to settle down. I want to get away from Savannah. Far, far, away. I want the divorce to finally go through so I can get on with my life. I always wanted a big family. I wanted to be a young father. She's sucking years of my life that should be spent with the woman I'm supposed to do that with. I want to be free of her so I can find the person I'm meant to spend my life with, the woman I can raise children with and share everything with." He turns back toward me, and his eyes are hot on mine, full of passion as he raises his voice a little. "And then you show up out of the blue after seven goddamn years and I'm just supposed to pretend like it *isn't* you when I've *known* it was you since I was twelve years old?"

Tears heat behind my eyes at his words, but a sudden question plays in my mind. "Can I ask you a question?"

He sits on my windowsill—in the same place I sit every night to talk to him. He's too far away, and yet he's closer than he's been for seven years. "Anything."

"If you knew it was me since we were twelve, why didn't you fight to find me when I left?" I know why I didn't fight to find him. I *couldn't*. I didn't have a way to get in touch with him, and then the baby came. I was emotionally damaged by that point, and I just wanted to climb out of the pit I'd been forced into. I had to rebuild my life, and while I wanted to rebuild it with him, by the time I was able to find some way to track him down, he was in season. He'd moved on without me, and I couldn't find it in my heart to pull him backward with me. Not when he was set on a path toward greatness.

He averts his gaze to the ground. "I tried. Believe me. I begged your father more than once, but he told me you didn't want to be with me anymore, that you'd asked him to end it with me. I tried your mom, too, because I didn't believe his story, not when I believed so strongly in *us*. This one time it felt like she was going to tell me something, but your dad walked in, and she had this look on her face like she'd been caught."

A tear tips over my lashes and onto my cheek as I think about what my father actually did to me. It hurts, and maybe it makes it even worse that he's gone now, that I can't confront him or punish him or eventually find a way to forgive him.

"For a long time, I thought it had to be something I did—that you left on your own free will, that you really didn't want to be with me anymore like he said," he says, resting his elbows on his knees and leaning forward as he folds his hands in front of him. "But I knew what we had, and I knew that wasn't the case. There was some reason they hated me, some reason they didn't trust me with you. They thought I was corrupting you, I wasn't good enough for you, or whatever. And then I had to leave for college, where I was immersed in football."

He rubs his hands together as he narrates that time in his life. "I had a receiver coach who saw my potential to make it to the NFL, and he basically only let me out of workouts and conditioning to attend classes or do my schoolwork. Otherwise, I was studying film and learning from the greats so I could become one of the greats. And that was it. The next time I heard a word about you, you were dating some guy in the city and he was maybe going to ask you to marry him. And you know where that led me from there."

I nod. "I'm sorry. I'm sorry my parents—my *father*—ever made you feel like you were anything less than the incredible person you are. I'm sorry my father made you doubt what we had for even a second."

"Did you try to get in touch with me?" he asks.

The answer to that question is complicated, but I keep it simple. "Of course I did, but my aunt was as strict as my father, and you're right. He didn't want me to be with you. Not because he didn't like you or didn't trust you, but because he suspected we were having sex and he didn't approve. He wanted to find a way to get me away from you, and so he forced me to leave the final quarter of senior year. I missed prom, graduation, time with you…everything that was important to me. He took it all away, and I hate him. I hate that he's gone, that he escaped so easily, that I can't hate him while he's still here and that he can't feel that hate. I hate that I have to pretend like I forgive him when I don't. He took away everything I held precious, and I'm not the same person I was before."

He stands and crosses the room, and he holds out his hands to me. I set mine in his, and he helps me lift to a stand. He wraps his arms around me and buries his face in my neck. After a beat of an embrace, I feel his lips on my skin, and then I hear his whispered words. "You're still the same person you were, and together, we're still dynamite. I still love you, Tessa. That never stopped."

"I still love you, too," I whisper, and his lips collide with mine.

CHAPTER 5

Tristan

"I told my parents," he says softly.

"What did they say?" I tug the blanket up around my stomach. The weather is starting to warm up a little, but the nights are still chilly beside an open window…or maybe the chill I'm feeling comes from the fear that his parents know.

More people are finding out.

It only makes things more real…and it only presents a bigger risk of more people finding out who the real father is.

"A lot of things," he mutters. "My mom was surprised your mom kept it from her."

"She did it at my request. It's not that I was lying to anybody or anything…I just wasn't ready to talk about it." I clear my throat as emotion seems to clog it for a beat. "I'm still not. It's embarrassing that it happened the way it did. And it's like…people know I have *sex*." I whisper the last word.

"There's nothing shameful about that, Tess, despite what your father tried to make you believe." His voice is low as he says the words, but I realize how much my religion was drilled into me from a young age. I started to shed some of those beliefs as I took on my independence in Chicago—as I moved out of my father's restrictive shadow—but knowing what he did in his free time despite what he tried to teach me has really sent my morality meter into total chaos.

Tristan was raised so differently than me. His house was sex positive, where it was a taboo subject in mine. And yet…he's not the one who's having a baby out of wedlock. Just because his family talked about it doesn't mean he sleeps around, and just because mine didn't doesn't mean I acted out of rebellion to get to where I am.

"I know," I mumble as I study my blanket so I don't feel his eyes burning into me…judging me.

"Hey," he says softly. I glance over at him, and his eyes are genuine as they stare at me. Not judgmental.

"What?"

"It's okay. It might not be how you imagined things, but you're not alone. Okay?"

I nod. "Okay."

But that's kind of the thing. Maybe I'm not alone right now, but I *will be*. He's a young, very attractive, successful celebrity. He can have his pick of whoever he wants in the entire world, and somehow I doubt that's the girl next door who's about to become a single mother. He'll need to go back to Vegas at some point, and then what?

He must be able to tell from my single word response that I'm not convinced.

He stands, disappears for a few seconds—presumably to grab his shoes—then opens his window. The very second he stood, I knew what he planned to do, and my hunch is correct. He climbs through his window, and just like old times, he skips the few steps across the yard separating us and opens my window wider. I move off my windowsill, and he climbs into my bedroom.

Now *this*…this feels like old times.

I can't help a breathless laugh as he takes me into his arms. "You're not alone," he repeats. He leans his forehead to mine.

"I know." I hear it in my own voice, so I'm sure he detects it, too. Fear.

"Then what are you scared of?" he whispers.

I pull out of his arms and move toward my bed to sit. "This is nice now, but I'm having a baby, Tristan. A baby that isn't yours, and you're still married to someone else. Even if you're here for me, even if the things I didn't even dare to dream actually come true and somehow we end up back together—which I can't even ask of you given that I'm pregnant with somebody else's child—eventually you'll have to go back to Vegas. You'll have to go back to your life, and you *should* go back to your life. You deserve to. You don't deserve to be tied down to some ex-girlfriend because you feel some sense of responsibility to make up for the past."

He presses his lips together. "Is that what you think this is?"

I shrug and hold up my hands as if to say, *prove me wrong*.

He shakes his head, and I think I sense a little disgust in the action.

"What?" I challenge.

He sighs as he averts his eyes over toward the window. "It's not obligation. It's not responsibility."

"Then what?" I ask, a desperate, pleading quality clouding my voice.

He shakes his head before he turns back toward me. He paces a little as he speaks. "It's love, Tessa Taylor. Pure, plain, and simple. We might've just been teenagers, but we had something special."

He stops pacing and he turns to face me. "Maybe I held you up on some pedestal after you walked out of my life, but I knew it wasn't because of you. I knew there was something else at play, something you didn't tell me, something you *couldn't* tell me, maybe, something I'm not even sure I want you to tell me at this point because it's in the past and I don't think it matters anymore."

My breath catches in my throat as he refers to that time, and a sense of relief falls onto my shoulders at his words. He's giving me permission not to tell him what happened. It feels freeing at the same time it feels…weird.

"You're pregnant, and that baby you're growing deserves to be your focus. We're here now. We found our way back, somehow, some way, and I think it's because it's fate." He sighs as he turns toward the window. "All I've been thinking about over the last few months is how I want to settle down. I want to get away from Savannah. Far, far, away. I want the divorce to finally go through so I can get on with my life. I always wanted a big family. I wanted to be a young father. She's sucking years of my life that should be spent with the woman I'm supposed to do that with. I want to be free of her so I can find the person I'm meant to spend my life with, the woman I can raise children with and share everything with." He turns back toward me, and his eyes are hot on mine, full of passion as he raises his voice a little. "And then you show up out of the blue after seven goddamn years and I'm just supposed to pretend like it *isn't* you when I've *known* it was you since I was twelve years old?"

Tears heat behind my eyes at his words, but a sudden question plays in my mind. "Can I ask you a question?"

He sits on my windowsill—in the same place I sit every night to talk to him. He's too far away, and yet he's closer than he's been for seven years. "Anything."

"If you knew it was me since we were twelve, why didn't you fight to find me when I left?" I know why I didn't fight to find him. I *couldn't*. I didn't have a way to get in touch with him, and then the baby came. I was emotionally damaged by that point, and I just wanted to climb out of the pit I'd been forced into. I had to rebuild my life, and while I wanted to rebuild it with him, by the time I was able to find some way to track him down, he was in season. He'd moved on without me, and I couldn't find it in my heart to pull him backward with me. Not when he was set on a path toward greatness.

He averts his gaze to the ground. "I tried. Believe me. I begged your father more than once, but he told me you didn't want to be with me anymore, that you'd asked him to end it with me. I tried your mom, too, because I didn't believe his story, not when I believed so strongly in *us*. This one time it felt like she was going to tell me something, but your dad walked in, and she had this look on her face like she'd been caught."

A tear tips over my lashes and onto my cheek as I think about what my father actually did to me. It hurts, and maybe it makes it even worse that he's gone now, that I can't confront him or punish him or eventually find a way to forgive him.

"For a long time, I thought it had to be something I did—that you left on your own free will, that you really didn't want to be with me anymore like he said," he says, resting his elbows on his knees and leaning forward as he folds his hands in front of him. "But I knew what we had, and I knew that wasn't the case. There was some reason they hated me, some reason they didn't trust me with you. They thought I was corrupting you, I wasn't good enough for you, or whatever. And then I had to leave for college, where I was immersed in football."

He rubs his hands together as he narrates that time in his life. "I had a receiver coach who saw my potential to make it to the NFL, and he basically only let me out of workouts and conditioning to attend classes or do my schoolwork. Otherwise, I was studying film and learning from the greats so I could become one of the greats. And that was it. The next time I heard a word about you, you were dating some guy in the city and he was maybe going to ask you to marry him. And you know where that led me from there."

I nod. "I'm sorry. I'm sorry my parents—my *father*—ever made you feel like you were anything less than the incredible person you are. I'm sorry my father made you doubt what we had for even a second."

"Did you try to get in touch with me?" he asks.

The answer to that question is complicated, but I keep it simple. "Of course I did, but my aunt was as strict as my father, and you're right. He didn't want me to be with you. Not because he didn't like you or didn't trust you, but because he suspected we were having sex and he didn't approve. He wanted to find a way to get me away from you, and so he forced me to leave the final quarter of senior year. I missed prom, graduation, time with you…everything that was important to me. He took it all away, and I hate him. I hate that he's gone, that he escaped so easily, that I can't hate him while he's still here and that he can't feel that hate. I hate that I have to pretend like I forgive him when I don't. He took away everything I held precious, and I'm not the same person I was before."

He stands and crosses the room, and he holds out his hands to me. I set mine in his, and he helps me lift to a stand. He wraps his arms around me and buries his face in my neck. After a beat of an embrace, I feel his lips on my skin, and then I hear his whispered words. "You're still the same person you were, and together, we're still dynamite. I still love you, Tessa. That never stopped."

"I still love you, too," I whisper, and his lips collide with mine.

CHAPTER 6

Tessa

I read the text message again as I sit at my kitchen table, cross-checking my lists and making sure I have everything in order for the fair. Mrs. Asher was all too willing to have Fallon Ridge High School students write the application essays for the festival funds, and I've been reviewing them all day. She only gave me the top twenty, but Landon's is the best so far. He's a hard worker deserving of a break, and I'm hopeful that Tristan and I can help give him one.

In addition to the essays, I've taken over my mother's garage, and tables are filled with donated items for the auction and raffles out there. Sue is working on making raffle baskets, and we're less than two weeks out. I feel organized, and yet I feel like it's all happening too fast and there are a million details to take care of.

Stephanie: *I decided to organize a craft fair to benefit Kewanee! Let's chat so we can share ideas.*

First…what?

And second…*what?*

Why is she doing this?

It's like she's copying everything I'm doing. First the weird Instagram pictures, which I never told anyone about, and then our conversation about her studying to become a nurse, and now…this.

Next thing you know she'll show up pregnant.

I sigh as I try to figure out how to handle this one.

Me: *We're in the final stretch now over here. Lots of last-minute details to cover so now isn't a good time for me but we can chat soon.*

I realize I should've left off that last part as soon as I send it. I'm committing to a future conversation when all I want is to keep this person at arm's length…or better yet, to get her out of my life completely.

The doorbell rings, and I lift to a stand as I hope I know who it is. I see his face through the tempered glass of the window in the door, and he grins when I open it. He's wearing a baseball cap backwards on his head again, and my knees nearly give out at how freaking hot he looks.

He takes me into his arms like we've been apart for weeks rather than under twelve hours, and he presses a quick, soft kiss to my lips.

My chest aches for more.

But that's where I'm at right now. This is where I've put us.

We're sort of together but not really—we can't *really* be together yet. We've kissed a few times, but to me…it can't lead any further than that for now. But as soon as I know he's free, well, the gates will unlock and the angels will sing.

Or something like that.

I'm a few steps beyond self-conscious about the current shape of my body. My stomach seems to have popped overnight, like it was waiting for me to tell Tristan about the baby so it could let loose, and I went from being able to hide the bump to feeling like I'm about seventeen months pregnant.

Okay, that's a *bit* of an exaggeration, but I woke up with a fresh new pain in my hip and my feet are getting harder and harder to see. Or to reach.

Tristan sets a hand on my tummy as if to tell the baby good morning, too, and it's about the sweetest thing I can imagine. I'm wearing a t-shirt today, glad I don't need to hide my belly anymore because frankly the big sweatshirts were starting to get hot. I'm hot all the time, in fact, which is why I'm currently wearing a pair of shorts with one of those belly bands built in paired with a maternity shirt that says *Spoiler Alert: It's a Girl*.

His eyes meet mine and he offers a soft smile, and I'm still so torn on how to feel about his attention. It's my baby…but I want to share her with the man I love. I want her to be *ours*, but I also don't want to hold a young, attractive, single man back from all the joys he deserves out of life.

Unless having a child is the joy he wants right now. It seems to be—and by some miracle, he seems to want it with *me*—but I don't want to feel like I'm holding him back in any way.

And yet, that feeling permeates my chest. It crawls up my spine, seeps into my veins and swims in my blood.

The last thing I want is for him to be with me out of obligation. He assured me last night that wasn't it…and I should take him at his word. Still, the thought plagues me, among others. The spotlight, for one. The fact that our life together would be very public when I have not one but two secrets that are vital to keep under wraps for very different reasons.

I keep thinking we can cross that bridge when we get to it, but maybe we're there.

I close the door behind him and we start on our path toward the table, where we're planning to knock out whatever we can for the fair.

"Is your mom home?" he asks.

I shake my head. "She's at the church but she's been working on the carnival games. One side of the garage is a mess of auction and raffle items, and the other side is full of supplies."

He chuckles. "I need to figure out some way to thank our biggest volunteers. Maybe a pizza party at the Joint in a few weeks or something." He rolls the idea around as we each take a seat. "I was hoping I could get my buddy Ben Olson to stop by, but he's getting married the weekend before the event. It's all hush hush and he's doing it up in Montana."

"Are you going?" I ask, a little alarmed that he might not be in town the weekend before our event.

He shakes his head. "No, they're doing it super privately so the media doesn't show up. But if I was invited, I'd bring you as my date." He winks at me.

He's in the spotlight now, and I'd be the mystery pregnant woman by his side. He's going through a divorce, and most certainly questions would arise as to who he's spending his time with and who fathered the child of the mystery woman on his arm—because if he's supposedly been faithful to his wife, then the baby I'm carrying couldn't possibly be his.

I blow out a breath. "I'd want to go. I'd love to meet your friends and see what your life is like now, not to mention what a dream it would be to meet the NFL stars…but it wouldn't be a good idea. The timing is just…not ideal."

His brows dip. "You want to meet NFL stars? You do realize one is literally sitting less than a foot away from you and wants to strip you naked and fuck you on this kitchen table until you can't see straight, right?"

My eyes widen at his words. I suck in a breath as a needy ache lands squarely between my thighs. "I can't believe you just said that."

He leans in a little closer and lowers his voice. "I've changed, too, Tessa. I'm not the boy whose fingers trembled as they got close to your breast. I haven't slept around, exactly, but I know what I'm doing, and I'd be happy to show you how I've…matured."

I pick up a sheet of paper on the table and use it to fan myself. He certainly isn't a boy anymore, and the more time we spend together, the more I can't wait for him to prove it.

"Is it warm in here?" I ask, and the tremble in my voice is a contrast to the thing he just said.

He chuckles. "I'm always hot when I'm around you."

I'm trying to come up with some witty reply—or trying to find a way to change the subject—when the doorbell rings again.

"Excuse me," I say, and I practically run to answer the door.

His laugh echoes behind me, and I get the sense he finds more than a little bit of joy in flirting with me…and in saying things that take me completely by surprise.

And speaking of taking me completely by surprise, when I open the door, my jaw drops a little at who's standing there. I blink once, and then again, just to make sure I'm not seeing things. "Stephanie," I say. "What are you doing here?"

She doesn't answer my question but instead steps into the house uninvited and hugs me. She steps back a little, eyeing my stomach. "Are you…" she trails off, not finishing her question, but my spoiler alert shirt pretty much says it all.

Her eyes are wide as they move from my stomach back up to my face, and I finally nod.

"Is it Tristan's?" she asks quietly.

I raise both brows. I have no idea how to answer that. It's not, and yet…he's made it seem as though he wants it to be. Does he?

"I'm sorry…but why are you here?" I ask, tilting my head as my brows knit together.

"You mentioned you were getting close to the finish line, so I just dropped by to see if I could help at all." She smiles, and there's something a little off about that smile as I pair it with the fact that it would be impossible for her to *just drop by*. Fallon Ridge isn't the type of place anybody just drops by. It's close to the highway, sure, but it's still a ten-minute trek to get to my house from there. The only reason someone *might* get off at our exit is to grab a tank of gas, but somehow I don't believe that's what Stephanie is doing here.

She looks past me toward the kitchen table where Tristan is sitting watching us.

She narrows her eyes as she looks at him then back at me as if she just noticed he's here. I spot a little something in her eyes…jealousy, maybe? Is she jealous I'm spending time with him? "Oh, sorry. Am I interrupting something?"

Yes, in fact, you are.

"We're working on some final details for the festival," I say. "I'm sorry, but now isn't a good time." I say it gently, and the way her face immediately hardens tells me that isn't what she wanted to hear.

"Oh," she says. "I see." She doesn't budge for a beat, and Tristan must sense my desperation to get rid of her because he stands and saunters over.

"I don't know if we've been properly introduced. I'm Tristan." He holds out his hand to shake hers, and she looks a little intimidated by him.

As someone who has known him since we were twelve, I know he's one of the least intimidating people I've ever met. He's kind and compassionate, and he'll help pretty much anybody with anything if he has the means to help.

But a stranger like Stephanie would see something else entirely. A tall man at six feet, five inches, and I have no idea what he weighs, but he's lean and muscular.

And he's hot as fuck. Dark hair that's usually styled nearly in a messy faux hawk—but a little messier, a little more blended, and not quite as long on top as the style might call for, but today it's covered with that baseball cap. Dark eyes that don't hide his emotions. A little bit of scruff on his jaw today that ups the hotness factor a bit. A body beneath the t-shirt and jeans that looks like it's cut from marble. And he's a professional athlete in a sport that creates celebrities out of its players.

It's all about perspective, I guess. He's not intimidating to me, but I've also been in love with him half my life.

"I know who you are," she says, and unlike Tristan who doesn't really hide his emotions, I can't quite get a read on what she's thinking. Her tone doesn't convey what it is, exactly, but I think I'm sensing desire.

Who wouldn't desire this man?

He's a catch and a half.

And somehow…he wants *me*.

CHAPTER 7

Tristan

"It's nice meeting you," I say. "Tessa and I were just heading out."

Tessa's eyes edge over to me. "Oh, right. I need to grab my shoes and coat." She clears her throat, and I think she's nervous to leave her half-sister alone with me.

Stephanie stands there, clearly oblivious to our social cues that she should just leave. I could see how uncomfortable Tessa was as she stood near the entry with her half-sister, so I decided to craft some way to get her to leave. We don't *need* to go anywhere, but it wouldn't hurt to take a quick walk down Main Street so we can visualize where everything is going to go.

And I have another place in mind, too.

I give Tessa a little nod, and she skips down the hallway toward her bedroom.

"Thanks for stopping by to check if we needed any help, but we've got it covered. It'll be a busy couple weeks leading up to the festival," I say, dropping another hint, but I get the feeling I need to be direct here.

Something about this woman makes me wonder whether she's a little off her rocker. Maybe it's the way her eyes dart around as if she's taking in every detail. Maybe it's the way they land on me like she's making some accusation I haven't quite put together yet.

"Right," she says flatly. "I suppose you two will be spending all your time together."

My brows dip. "I'm sorry, but I'm not sure what business that is of yours."

She raises her brows and takes a step back as if I just issued a physical blow. "She's my *sister*."

"Your *half*-sister," I correct.

She narrows her eyes at me into a glare. "We share a father. I just want to get to know her, but you're always hogging her." Her voice lowers, and I get the feeling the waterworks are about to begin. She's starting to remind me a little of someone else I know who's completely off her rocker.

My wife.

"It's a difficult situation, Stephanie, and I think Tessa just needs some time to process everything she's learned about her father," I say, going for the gentlest possible tone. "*Your* father."

She purses her lips, and thankfully Tessa reappears a beat later. "Ready," she announces, a little breathless as she must've grabbed shoes and a coat at record speed.

"I guess I'll be going, too, then. I'll see you soon," Stephanie says.

All three of us walk toward the door, and once we're outside and Tessa locks the deadbolt, Stephanie pauses in the driveway.

"It was great seeing you again," she says, tossing her arms around Tessa. "Congratulations on the baby. Whoever it belongs to."

Tessa deflates a little at her jab, but fuck that.

"It's not your business," I say tightly.

She pulls out of her hug with my girl and purses her lips. "Tessa can tell me that."

Tessa tugs her coat more tightly around her even though it's not that cold out here. She licks her lips and shifts on her feet, clearly uncomfortable with this conversation. Her eyes edge over to me. "I'm just keeping things quiet for now."

"Well, we're off," I say, and I grab Tessa's hand and lead her toward the sidewalk. "Bye."

Tessa yells a goodbye over her shoulder, too, and we start walking toward town. I don't toss a glance behind my shoulder to see what Stephanie is up to, but her car goes whizzing past us just as we turn the corner onto Main Street.

Tessa lets out a breath she must've been holding since she yelled that goodbye.

"What's up with that girl?" I ask.

She shrugs and shakes her head. "No clue. She drops by unannounced when this isn't a convenient place to just drop by, she makes little comments that only serve to piss me off, and I think she might be a little on the crazy side. Oh, and she's totally, completely in love with you and jealous that I'm spending time with you."

My jaw slackens and I stop walking at her words. Is that really what she thinks? "Are you serious?"

She drops my hand and turns to face me, her brows knit together in confusion at my reaction. "What?"

"You seriously think she's in love with me?"

She raises both brows and holds up her hands as if to say, *well, prove me wrong.*

I shake my head a little. "She's not in love with me."

"You didn't see the jealousy in her eyes when she saw that you were there and I was spending time with you?" she asks.

"Oh, I saw it," I say, nodding. "She's jealous of *me* for spending time with *you*. You know what she said to me when you went to get your coat?"

"What?"

I grab her hand and we resume our walk. "She said I'm hogging you. She doesn't want me. She wants you."

Tessa sighs. "Well now I feel bad."

I chuckle. "Don't. There's something off about her, and I don't like that she drops by unannounced. She's veiling something with wanting to get to know her sister, but she's got some of the same traits Savannah has and it's both toxic and scary."

"Terrifying," she murmurs, and she pauses a beat. "I, uh, never told you this. I haven't said anything to anyone, actually, but you saying she wants time with me, she's jealous of you…"

I stop walking again as alarm creeps over me. "What is it?" We're standing in the middle of the sidewalk on Main Street. It's quiet on a weekday late morning. Everyone's at work or school, but every now and again a car drives by and we stop to wave.

"I saw her Instagram page the other day, and it was filled with photos that were…familiar. Photos I'd taken with my dad at random places that meant something to us, only my dad wasn't in them and neither was I. It was like she was standing in the exact same place I was in each of the images," she says. "I don't know, maybe I was imagining things. I got freaked out and stopped looking."

"Show me," I say.

She pulls her phone out of her pocket and navigates to Instagram and then to Stephanie's profile. She shows me a few pictures.

"I don't know why she would be in Maple Park," she says, and she scrolls through some more. Then she pulls open Facebook and navigates to her father's profile. She sucks in a breath as she scrolls to some of the older photographs—ones posted more than a decade ago, even before she moved to Fallon Ridge.

And sure enough, the evidence is right in front of us. The hairs on the back of my neck stand at attention. "What the fuck?" I murmur as I look at the images of a young Tessa next to her father in front of the pumpkin farm…the exact same photo Stephanie posted not so long ago. And the Dairy Mart, and the house in Maple Park, and the Methodist Church…photo after photo that's a carbon copy of ones Tessa took with her dad. "It's like she's trying to *be* you."

"She told me she's going to school for her nursing degree, and she decided to plan a craft fair for her hometown where she still lives. Next thing you know she'll show up pregnant and dating a football player." She laughs, but then she slaps a hand over her mouth.

"What?" I ask.

She shifts awkwardly on her feet and snags her bottom lip between her teeth. "Oh, I uh…um—we just…" She shakes her head and holds a hand over her eyes like she's mortified. "I just said we're dating. Are we dating?"

"You won't let me date you until my divorce is finalized," I remind her, and then I pull her hand from her eyes. "But we're definitely doing something here, Tessa. I think it's safe to say there's nobody else for me."

"But I'm pregnant with another man's baby," she whisper yells.

I nod and press my lips together. "I know. And it doesn't matter. I want to be with you *and* the baby. I want to get the fuck away from Savannah so we can be together. I want to raise that baby with you, if you'll let me, and I want to make a life with you and her and however many more kids we're blessed with. And a dog. And a white picket fence." We both look across the street at the house on the corner.

It's a gorgeous two-story white house with a balcony and a wraparound porch built in the Colonial style, and outlining the entire property is the white picket fence. It's probably the biggest house in Fallon Ridge, and it's situated on the corner of Main Street and Weeping Willow Lane. Just a block down Main Street to the north sits our downtown area, and a few blocks to the south is the high school.

Tessa loves this house. She's always loved it.

When we were young, we'd walk by it and she'd tell me how someday she wanted to live there. It's on a huge corner lot, so it has a nice yard for entertaining and the owners, Mr. and Mrs. Cunningham, have kept it up beautifully over the years. They had two kids, each a few years older than Tessa and me, and now the Cunninghams are empty nesters with grandchildren who live in different cities.

Maybe someday…

She rushes into my arms, and I simply hold her for a few beats.

"What did I ever do to deserve someone as good as you?" she asks into my chest.

"I often wonder the same thing about you," I say, and I press a soft kiss to the top of her head.

We continue our trek toward town and spend the next hour pointing out where tables and booths and games and food are going to go. We've got a good handle on things, but it helps to look at the space itself instead of at a piece of paper with a sketch on it.

After we're done, I glance at my watch and then over at Tessa. "You up for a short walk?"

She nods, and my fingers link through hers as we walk down Main Street a bit then turn toward the east side of town.

She doesn't ask where we're going, but it's pretty obvious once we start heading east. We walk past the rows of houses, past the cornfields, along the river's edge, and then we walk down the short dock leading to the scenic overlook.

Honest **MISTAKE**

We sit together on one of the benches looking out over the water—our favorite bench. The one where I asked her to go to the Homecoming dance with me when I knew I felt like we were turning into much more than friends. The one where I asked her to the prom our senior year that we never got to go to. The one where we spent hours talking about what we wanted out of our shared future as we stared out over the water.

There were a lot of places in this town I'd consider *ours*, but maybe none more than this bench. We had our booth at the Pizza Joint. We had our tree in the park, the one where I carved T and T. I spot the T plus T carved into the bench here, too, and think for a second what a little vandal I was just carving our letters into any wooden surface.

There are others, too—high school couples in love who came before us and after us. We weren't alone.

I wonder if any of them are still together.

I wonder if any of them reconnected the way we're trying to.

I wonder if any of them were ripped apart the way we were.

In some instances, I don't *have* to wonder. Jennifer and Chris didn't make it the long haul. Jamie married Andy, and they already have two kids with the third on the way. I spot the J plus K and I know Jake and Kayla broke up two days after he carved it into the wood of our bench.

But none of them matter.

All that matters is I'm here with my girl again.

She wraps both her arms around one of mine, rests her head on my shoulder, and draws in a deep breath before exhaling, like she's letting go of all her worries, releasing them into the river.

I do the same.

We don't tarnish the silent comfort of this place with words today. Instead, we each take something we need from this place that holds so many memories, and a short while later, we head back to Tessa's house.

"Want lunch?" she asks.

"I'm meeting my dad for lunch in Davenport, and I have some things to take care of in town. I need to head out, but I'll be at the window tonight."

"I'll be there." She smiles, and there's something really special about being back in the place where we can count on seeing each other at the window.

CHAPTER 8

"So are we back together or what?"

That's the question I *want* to ask as I sit on my windowsill across from her, but we're in this confusing state of flux where I'm waiting on a call from my lawyer to give me permission to be with the woman I actually want to be with.

So I don't ask it.

Yet.

She slipped earlier and said we were dating, and I'm taking that as good enough for now.

"I have a doctor's appointment on Wednesday," she says. She clears her throat and glances at me a little nervously. "My mom has a meeting she can't get out of, so I'm going alone if you want to come." Her voice is soft, like she's imposing on my free time by even asking.

"You're not going alone," I say, my voice louder and confident. "Of course I want to come."

Her brows dip a little as she tugs on the hem of the blanket covering her legs. "Can I ask you a question?"

"Anything."

"Why are you being so good to me?"

I draw in a breath as I consider her question for a beat. I'm living on instinct here, doing the things I feel are the right things to do despite others—including my own parents—trying to talk me out of it.

I want to be with Tessa.

They say when you know, you know, and I've *always* known it was her.

I made mistakes, I dipped my feet into other waters, I stayed married to Savannah longer than I should have since I didn't have Tessa to give me the motivation I needed to get the fuck out, but no matter what I've been through since she left…it always comes back to her.

"Because we're T and T," I finally say. She chuckles a little, but I shake my head, dead serious. "I mean it, Tess. We're Tristan and Tessa. We have a history that binds us, but we have this indescribable bond that doesn't just go away, you know? We ended up in the same place after seven years apart and we picked up right where we left off."

"If I hadn't shown up at the same time as you, do you think we would've found our way back to each other?" she asks.

"I know we would have." I press my lips together. "Fate would have intervened in some other way. It would have stepped in to push us back together. I can't say how or when, but you and me? We're destined to end up together. It's as simple and as complicated as that. Maybe it would've been another seven years before it happened. Maybe you'd have kids, maybe I'd be long divorced, who the hell knows what might've changed in all that time. But one thing's for certain: at some point, our lives would've crossed again. We would've found our way back to where we belong."

"But I'm pregnant," she says, as if her argument will scare me off or drive me away.

Nothing could scare me off from her.

Nothing.

"I know." My voice is soft. "It doesn't matter who has that baby's DNA. If I'm with you, if we're together, married, whatever…I will raise that child as my own. You have everything I want out of life, including that baby girl. It's like some giant puzzle board up in the heavens where the angels match the pieces together, and somehow, your pieces click in perfectly with mine."

Her eyes get a little misty at that description. "Really?" she asks softly. "You want all this?" She gestures down her body to indicate her pregnant stomach, and her hand lands on her chest to indicate herself.

I climb out of my window because she doesn't seem to be getting it from words alone.

She scoots over to make room for me, and the two of us sit on her windowsill once I'm in. I toss an arm around her shoulders, and I press a soft kiss to her temple. "I want *all* of it. Doctor's appointments and craft fairs and corn boils and football games and two AM feedings and diapers and trikes and fishing on the river. A life here and a life in Vegas. And I want to support whatever it is *you* want to do, too. You want to find a job nursing again? Let's scan the internet. You want to plan festivals? Let's plan. You want to be a stay at home mom? Let's get some yoga pants, flip flops, and a whole lot of coffee. Is that what stay at home moms need?"

She laughs even as she wipes a tear from her eyes. "Somehow you always know the exact right thing to say."

"Oh, I don't know about that," I say modestly. I'm sure my *wife* would disagree with that statement, but I don't want to bring her up when Tessa and I are having such a warm moment together.

She leans into my chest, and then she tilts her head back. I take it as an invitation, and I tilt my head down to press a soft kiss to her lips. I move to back away, to keep it short and simple, but she's not having it. She grabs my face between her fingertips, opening her mouth to mine, and a rush of emotions plows into me. She swings her leg over so she's straddling my lap, one leg on either side of me as I sit on her windowsill.

Our kiss moves from slow to intense as our tongues batter against each other, and kissing her now is even better than kissing her back then was. Maybe because we're all grown up now, because we've weathered the storm and ended up on the other side of it, because we've each been through some things and we came out okay.

She shifts her hips down over me, and my dick hardens painfully with need. She moves her hands from my face as she wraps her arms around my neck, and I wrap my arms around her waist, my hands reaching under her shirt to skate along the porcelain skin of her back.

I pull her body close against me, as close as we can get, and I'm more turned on than I've ever been in my entire life.

I don't just *want* her. I *need* her. I *crave* her.

I love her.

Every single piece of her. The past, the present, and, with any luck, the future.

She shifts again over me, and then she pulls back, her eyes cloudy with lust. "How much longer until that divorce is finalized?"

I let out a soft chuckle as disappointment lances through me. "According to my lawyer, uncontested divorces can go through in as little as one to three weeks in Nevada depending on how full the docket is."

"Then let's hope for an empty docket."

Let's hope indeed.

Once I'm back in my room all alone, my phone starts to ring.

Savannah.

Against my better judgment, I pick up. Call it fear of what she might do if I don't.

"What?" I answer.

"I signed the papers," she says quietly. "It's uncontested, but it's not too late to stop this from going through. Can't we just…find a way to work it out?"

I can't help my laugh. She's up to something, and that's for damn sure. "No, Savannah. We tried. I gave it two years, and you gave me nothing but hell. I'm done. I'm ready to move on with my life, and you should be, too."

Hell, she's an entire decade older than me.

Doesn't she want kids? A real marriage? Happiness?

I remember who she is as soon as those thoughts trespass my mind. She wants money. Fame. Access. She wants to be a football wife, and that's what matters to her above all else. I don't know why. I never cared to figure out her motivation, but somehow she managed to twist her way into not one, not two, but three football players' lives—not to mention Eric Scott, too. She'll move to a new city and start over. She'll make some other player's life hell.

But it won't be mine anymore.

She starts to say something, but I talk over her. "I wish you nothing but the best. Really. I hope you find the happiness you're searching for, but it can't be with me."

I hang up before she gets the chance to respond, and then I immediately open my photos. I glance through the papers I took photos of from her jewelry box, and none of it is extra shit on me. I recognize names of some high-powered businessmen in Las Vegas, and it would appear I'm not the only one she's been blackmailing.

While I hope and pray it's the last I hear from her, somehow I know it won't be.

CHAPTER 9

Tessa

We're on our way to my twenty-six week appointment when Tristan's phone starts ringing over his truck's Bluetooth system.

"Richard Redmond calling," the robotic female voice tells us.

He glances over at me. "I need to take this. It's my lawyer."

I nod, and he answers. "Hello, Richard."

He doesn't warn his lawyer that he's got somebody in the car with him, which only serves to build the trust between us. He doesn't care that I'm sitting here and listening to every word. Instead, he wants to share everything with me, and that means something big to me.

My chest warms and my heart squeezes as I sit quietly in the passenger seat.

"Tristan, I have good news for you for a change," Richard says.

"I'm listening."

"There's a benefit to holding residence in the state known for quickie divorces. It may have been two years in the making, but right now I hold in my hand your final divorce decree," Richard says, and I can't help when I squeal a little.

Tristan sinks back into the driver's seat, his shoulders moving down as if he'd been hunching them for two years with the weight of his mistake.

"Thank God," he murmurs.

"Well, I'm not God, but you're welcome anyway." Richard laughs.

"I can't believe it," Tristan says, wonder in his tone. "Can you send me a photo of it?"

"Already done, Tristan. It's waiting in your email. Congratulations."

"Thank you," he murmurs.

"Anything else I can do for you, you know how to get in touch," Richard says.

"Of course." Tristan ends the call then exhales a long, slow breath. He glances over at me with an eyebrow raised and a smile tipping the corners of his mouth.

"Congratulations," I say.

"Same to you," he replies, a hint of teasing in his tone.

"For what?" My brows crinkle as I try to imagine what he's getting at.

"For the best sex of your life that's about to happen."

I giggle. "It's about to happen? When?"

"Oh I have plans. Big ones."

When I look over at him, I can't help but wonder what he's got up his sleeve. But then I realize I don't really care.

We can finally be together, and that's all that matters. Whatever invisible barrier I put between us was plowed down with those finalized papers.

He pulls into a parking spot and grabs his phone once we arrive at the doctor's office, and he pulls open his email. He clicks the attachment, and he turns his phone toward me.

We stare at the picture of his divorce decree. I wonder what he's feeling right now as he looks at that piece of paper.

I know what I'm feeling. Hope. Excitement. Love. And a little bit of fear.

I have to admit even if it's just to myself that I'm a little scared of actually being with him again, and not just the spotlight and the fame and the money that come as part of his package.

I'm scared of it ending again. I'm scared that forces out of our control will signal the bitter end for us the same way they did the first time.

We're in a place now where we can fight back, but the notion of falling in love with him again, of really *being* with him again, only to have it ripped away…it's fresh at the forefront of my mind.

It's something I didn't really have to worry about until this very moment.

"How are you feeling?" I ask.

He blows out another breath, and he leans his head back on the headrest before turning his head toward me. His eyes are bright with hope when he says the single word: "Free."

He races around to my door to help me out, and he holds me in his arms for a beat as we stand between his truck and the car parked next to us. He presses a soft kiss to my lips.

He's free. I'm free. *We* are free. We can finally be together.

I just hope it's everything we both think it will be.

We head inside for the appointment, and I'm taken back to a room for my exam. Tristan sits in the chair in the corner, and when the tech comes in to take my vitals, he stands and holds my hand. She starts with my blood pressure, and then she rubs some gel on my stomach and uses a fetal doppler to listen for the heartbeat.

We don't hear anything for a beat as she pushes and adjusts the machine, and my chest tightens.

Is everything okay?

I feel this way every time, and eventually they find it.

But those five seconds of waiting are filled with fear.

My hands turn icy and Tristan's grip seems to strengthen.

And then we hear it. Swoosh-swoosh, swoosh-swoosh, swoosh-swoosh.

A sense of relief calms my chest, and I loosen my tight grip on Tristan's hand.

"One forty-two," she says, and Tristan glances at me.

"A hundred forty-two beats per minute. The normal range for right now is between one hundred forty and one hundred fifty," I explain.

"Is this your first time attending an appointment?" she asks him, and he nods. She smiles at him. "Baby is doing well, and so is Mama."

"Thank God for that," he says. He looks at me. "A day filled with great news." His eyes burn into mine, and it sends a dart of need through me.

Maybe it's weird, but suddenly I'm turned on at the doctor's office.

Thanks, Tristan.

The doctor comes in to check me out and assures me everything looks normal, and then I make my next appointment in four weeks and we're on our way.

"Do you have plans tonight?" Tristan asks on the way back toward Fallon Ridge.

I shake my head. "Just my usual nine fifty-seven meeting."

He chuckles. "Can I take you on an overnight date?"

"I would love that." I glance over at him a little nervously, and his eyes meet mine.

He reaches over to squeeze my hand, obviously sensing my nervousness. "What's wrong?"

"I just…" I draw in a breath. "My body, it's not, you know—it's not like it was when I was seventeen. I'm pregnant, and my stomach is huge and my boobs hurt and I'm a little self-conscious about what I look like right now."

His eyes soften as they turn back to the road. "Can I tell you something if you promise to believe every word I say?"

My brows knit together. "Okay…"

"You've never looked more beautiful to me, Tessa Taylor. I can't wait to take my time with that body. I can't wait to kiss every inch, to taste you, to touch you. Besides, I don't look like I did when I was seventeen, either."

"Yeah, but you've gotten firmer with age," I argue. "More athletic. More cut. I've gotten fat."

"You're not fat. Your body is doing the most incredible thing a body can do. You're creating life in there. I'm fascinated by that. It's fucking hot, babe. You have nothing to worry about. Trust me."

I wrinkle my nose. "You think I look *hot?*"

His eyes meet mine again before he turns back to the road, and I can see plainly written there the truth in his words before he even says them. "I think you are the most gorgeous woman I have ever laid eyes on."

"Thank you," I whisper, and suddenly, because of his words of praise, the negative thoughts in my own mind seem to quiet. They might not disappear altogether, but right now, seeing the way he looks at me, how he'll look at me when I'm naked and his for the taking, I know I will *feel* like a gorgeous woman simply because he sees me as one.

CHAPTER 10

Tessa

I text my mom when I get home.

Me: *Appointment went well! Baby is doing fine. I'm going out for the night and won't be back until morning. Love you!*

I decide not to fill her in on all the details. Obviously she knows I've had sex given the fact that I'm pregnant, but I don't need to warn her of my night's activities. Besides, when she sees Tristan's truck missing from the front of his house and my SUV still parked in the driveway, I'm pretty sure she'll put two and two together.

Whatever happens tonight, when I get back home tomorrow, I feel like Tristan and I will have defined whatever it is we have. We haven't needed to up to this point. I've been too busy pushing him away.

But now that his divorce is finalized, it's a totally different ballgame.

I pack an overnight bag, skipping the lingerie considering A, I don't own any, and B, my pregnant ass wouldn't fit into it even if I did, and just as I'm finishing up, I hear the familiar sound of stones hitting the wooden frame surrounding my window.

Good thing that kid always had decent aim.

I open my window, and my cheeks are flushed as I look ahead to our evening.

"You ready?" he asks.

I nod and offer a smile as a dart of nervousness sweeps through me.

He grins, and it only serves to increase those nerves.

God, he's hot. Was he always this hot? Because he is now, and I'm not sure we're playing in the same league—pregnant or not.

"Meet me out front," he says.

A chill runs up my spine at the way he demands it, and I can't help but think how I want him to demand other things of me, too.

He's sweet and kind, and he'll help anybody who needs help. But one thing I remember about our time together? He's not afraid to demand what he wants, and he's not afraid to simply ask for it, either. I remember that being a huge turn-on when we were together before. We were both inexperienced, learning together, and when he took the lead and told me what to do, or encouraged me by telling me what he liked, or told me to lie still because he wanted to try something…it was hot.

Like *super* hot.

While Cam demanded things and rode the line of being an arrogant asshole, I'd never mistake Tristan's confidence for arrogance.

And there was something different about Tristan that made what we shared so special, too—that made him the best sex of my life.

It was the very simple concept of love.

I've never loved anyone as hard as I loved him, and because of those deep feelings we shared, the sex was intimate and emotional every time—whether we were taking our time and exploring each other or if we had to be quick because our parents were only going to be out of the house for a short time.

As I sling my overnight bag on my shoulder and walk out of my bedroom to meet him out front, I can't help but pause. I turn and look at the bed as I think about the night we gave each other our virginity.

We didn't *lose* it to each other. It was something we shared, something we gave one another, something we both swore we wouldn't give anyone else until life happened and we did.

He'd been sneaking into my window for months so we could make out after Homecoming our sophomore year. Making out eventually shifted to over the shirt and over the pants touching, and eventually that shifted to moving under clothes and using hands and fingers, which transitioned to mouths exploring each other.

It was a year after we first officially got together. Homecoming night junior year. We'd danced after celebrating the football team's victory, and I was nervous the entire day. We ducked out early to head to my house.

We'd planned it. He asked me to the football field, of course, one day after practice. I had cheer, and I stayed late as he finished up on the field. He met me in the bleachers after practice, and we sat and talked as everyone else cleared the field.

"Can I ask you a question?" he asked me, and I nodded. "Have you thought about…you know. Sex? With me?"

"I think about it all the time," I breathed. I knew how he made me feel when we did those other things, and I knew sex with him was the next logical step. We'd talked about it before, but we'd skated around it. I was young at just sixteen, and I knew my parents wouldn't approve, but I wanted this. I wanted him. I wanted to be as close as two people could physically be, and I didn't care what anybody else thought.

I wanted to seal the love I felt for him by showing him how I felt with my body.

All our friends teased us relentlessly anyway. They assumed we were already doing it, not that either of us cared about their opinions. But the more they teased us, the more I wanted it.

There was no pressure in his question, and it was one of the things that made me feel even more ready to do it with him. He respected me, and I knew it would be special if it was with him.

"Homecoming night?" he asked. It was only a couple weeks away, and I would think of nothing else until the time came. "It's Bingo night. If we leave the dance a little early, we can go to my house or yours. Our parents won't be home."

"My house," I said immediately. I wanted those memories in my bed. On my sheets. I wanted to smell him long after he left.

He nodded, and then he leaned over and kissed my cheek.

And when the time finally came, it was perfect.

He took his time. He was gentle even though there were moments I could tell he didn't want to be. He made sure we were both enjoying it.

As time went on, we experimented. We tried different things. Harder, softer, faster, slower, gentler, rougher.

The *how* didn't matter. Every time was special because it was between the two of us, and as nervous as I am for tonight, I already know that in my heart.

This has been a long time coming—all of it. The date. The time we're going to have together. The night and everything that goes with it.

I'm ready.

And with that thought in mind, I practically run down the hall and out the front door toward Tristan's truck.

CHAPTER 11

Tristan

"You're stunning as always," I say. I'm leaning up against my truck waiting for her. Watching her practically skip toward me makes it feel like it's been worth the wait.

All seven years.

"Do you get hotter every day or is it my imagination?" She tilts her head as she studies me, and I laugh.

"I definitely get hotter every day."

God, am I ready for this night.

She reaches me and I take my foot off my truck to brace myself on both feet as I pull her into my arms. I press my lips to hers knowing full well that it's a mere preview of what's to come this evening.

I can't recall a time in our history together that we had this much uninterrupted time together. We were teenagers back then, which meant our parents could come home at any minute or friends would be interrupting us for something or any other of a multitude of things that come up in a teenager's life. We weren't old enough to get our own hotel room, not that her dad would've allowed something so scandalous anyway, but now we are…and I plan to use that to my advantage.

She pulls back. "What are your plans for us?"

"If I told you now it would ruin the surprise," I tease.

She pouts a little, but she's still in my arms and I know it's all in jest. "You know I've never really been one for surprises."

I laugh as I think back over the time we spent together. When we read books for English class, she'd read the last page first. When we watched a television show together, she'd search the internet for spoilers. It was something that both endeared her to me and drove me crazy.

She was always polite enough not to share the spoilers, but just knowing she knew what was going to happen sometimes made it not worth watching. I just wanted to make out with her, anyway. I was a horny teenager, and now I'm a horny adult.

"Hop in the truck and you'll find out soon enough," I say, opening the door for her and taking her bag from her shoulder. I toss it in back with mine, and for some reason the fact hits me that we're really doing this.

For as inseparable as we were back then, we really never got to spend the night with each other without the fear that our parents would catch us and we'd get in trouble. They knew how close we were, but it didn't really matter since we were teenagers…since she was the daughter of the town pastor. A lot of things stood in our way back then that just aren't issues today.

We went camping once with a big group of friends, but it wasn't like we could make love for hours in the sleeping bag with Jen and Chris sleeping in the tent next to us.

I did slip it in for a few seconds, though. It was tough in a sleeping bag, but we made it work.

I can't help a little smile at the memory.

I shut the door behind her and walk around to the driver's side. I fire up the engine and we're officially off on what I suppose is technically our first date even though it's also technically not at all.

Honest MISTAKE

I thought for a long time about where to take her and figured we'd want to start somewhere fun rather than somewhere that would create more tension between us. It was with that in mind that I chose our dinner destination. I thought about checking into the hotel first, but then I figured we'd never make it to dinner, and this boy's gotta eat. And I assume she needs to eat as well since she's pregnant, and I know once I get her naked, we won't be leaving our room until the sun comes up. Or later.

We pull into the parking lot of Capital Arcade in Davenport. It's a place we used to go when we were teenagers, but anyone under twenty-one had to leave by seven o'clock.

Tonight we'll leave early for other reasons, I'm sure.

I glance over to see if the look on her face tells me she approves of my dining selection, and she's grinning from ear to ear.

"I'm gonna kick your ass on the air hockey table," she announces.

"You think so, huh? Just like old times?" I tease. "As I recall, I went undefeated in our battles on the table."

"I may have brushed up on my air hockey skills in the last few years," she says, rubbing her knuckles on her shoulder.

I laugh. "Well I play against the pros now." In reality I'm referring to pro *football* players, not pro *air hockey* players.

She laughs. "We'll see if that matters."

We head inside and grab a couple seats at the bar in front of one of those arcade consoles with a bunch of different games.

We peruse the menu and the bartender comes over. We order drinks first, and she gets a Sprite. As much as I want some alcohol, I order a Coke…with no Jack in it.

A Jackless Coke.

"You can drink if you want to," she says, sensing that I'm not doing it because she can't.

I shake my head as the bartender walks away, and then I angle my head toward hers. "I need all of my faculties intact. I don't want to miss a single second of how it feels when I slide in your body later."

Her cheeks flush at my words, and I'm dying to see if her chest still flushes to match the red in her cheeks when she's turned on. I can't wait to watch as her nipples still tighten with the same need and desire as they used to, the way they always betrayed her when she wanted me. I want to know if she still tastes the same. These are the types of things you never forget about the first girl you ever loved…the only girl you ever loved.

The bartender drops off our sodas, and we order some food—chicken for me, naturally, and a burger and fries for her. I slide my credit card into the reader, and she flips through a menu of games.

"Spot the difference?" she asks.

I nod, and the game begins a minute later. We each tap on the screen as we work as a team to find all the differences in the first puzzle. Each level gets progressively more difficult and if we don't find a certain number of differences by the time our timer runs out, we lose.

Twenty bucks later, our food arrives.

She scarfs down her burger, and it's quite possibly the sexiest thing I've ever seen. She's comfortable with me, as comfortable as I am with her, and there's something insanely sexy about that. There are no pretenses between us, no faking it, no question as to whether she's only with me because I lucked into a career playing football.

It's only a small part of why my heart always wandered back to her, but it's an important part.

She wasn't there with me through college, or through the draft, or through my first three seasons. She was there before all that, and she still wants to be a part of my future.

We finish eating, and then we let our food settle a little over a round of air hockey.

"What are the stakes?" I ask.

Anytime we used to play, we'd make a bet—but it didn't matter who was actually the victor because we'd both end up the winners.

She thinks for a second, and then she says, "Winner gets to pick the position."

I laugh. "Deal."

"Best of three?" she asks.

"It'll only take two to put you away, babe."

She giggles. "We'll see."

She does give me a run for my money, but in the end, I win the first game.

I think about letting her win the second, but I think we're both ready for what comes next. Prolonging it with a third game will only delay the thing we're both looking forward to.

"You ready?" I ask after I win the second game.

She nods, and the way she looks up at me from lowered lashes seems to speak directly to my cock. She looks sweet and innocent…and while she can be, I also know she's not.

It's one of the things I remember about sex with her. She loved it when I'd tell her what to do. She loved it when I demanded things of her. There were times when the rougher I was, the wetter she became. She was vocal enough to tell me the things she liked—or the things she didn't like, though there were few of those—and she was adventurous enough to try pretty much anything.

I did a little research, and I found that the best positions for pregnant sex are doggy style and spoon style. I don't care which position we decide on…I'm just excited to have a player in the game.

I drive to the Blackhawk, the fanciest hotel in town. It's where we joked we'd get a room after our senior prom—always just a joke, though, since we knew our parents wouldn't spring for one for two underaged kids.

Not that it mattered anyway. She left and I didn't go to my senior prom.

I wonder if she did, wherever she ended up. I wonder what her graduation was like. I wonder a lot of things, but I also know they don't matter. I already told her I didn't want to know, and I stand by that.

"The Blackhawk?" she asks quietly once I pull into the parking lot.

"Felt like it had meaning, you know? We didn't get to do this back then."

She offers a soft smile when I glance over at her. "It's perfect."

I already checked in on the app, so I grab our bags from the back, and we bypass the front desk. We head right for our room—a corner suite that overlooks Davenport.

I open the door with the app on my phone and hold it open to allow her to go in first, and she flicks the light switch before walking across the room right for the windows. The view doesn't quite have the bright lights of the Vegas Strip, but it's got special meaning in its own way since it's the biggest town near where we grew up.

Somehow just pouncing on her doesn't seem right. We both know why we're here, but that doesn't mean we have to dive right in.

But she seems to have other ideas.

I walk over and slide my arm around her shoulders, and she leans into me.

"It's been a long time coming," she says quietly. "Are you ready?"

"I've been ready since the day you left, Tess. Everything else? Just a distraction, and not even any good ones."

She turns and looks up at me, a sad smile on her lips. "Same. I love you. I've always loved you." Her eyes sparkle with tears, and I lean my forehead down to hers.

"I love you, too."

She tilts her head to catch my lips with hers.

I lean down and turn into her, and she wraps her arms around my waist. I deepen the kiss, opening my mouth to hers, and time seems to stop as the only thing that matters is the collision of our mouths in this slow, luxurious kiss.

My fingers sink into her hair, the scent of jasmine wafting over to me and reminding me of everything I love about this woman. It's not just the tender kiss that's turning more and more needy by the second, but it's the way she steals my breath just by being in the same room as me. It's some intrinsic connection between the two of us, some abstract, intangible thing that links our souls together in a way nobody else has ever been able to touch.

Her lips become the oxygen I need to survive, and my body starts to move instinctually, my hips moving toward hers. A soft moan bubbles from her, a signal that she likes it and wants more.

I slowly move us over toward the couch I spotted in my pursuit of her when she stood by the window, and as her legs hit the back of it, she grabs onto my neck, pulling me down with her as we fall onto the soft surface. She lies back, propped by the armrest, and I thrust my hips to hers as she rocks along with me. Our limbs tangle together as we kiss like we used to. It's at once familiar and new, and then she wraps her legs around my torso and draws me in closer to her, moaning as she feels how hard I am for her.

How ready I am for her.

I pull back to look at her, and my eyes feast on the gorgeous face.

"I wish we would've found each other sooner," I say, and my fingertips brush along her jawline. I study her—the eyes a little cloudy with lust, the lips a little swollen with our passion, the cheeks a little flushed with need, and her eyes lock in on mine. "I wish we would've fought harder. I hate that so many years separated us, but we can't change the past. All we can do is focus forward."

"Let's make some new memories," she suggests, and then she pulls my head back down to hers.

CHAPTER 12

Tessa

I shift my hips again, desperate for friction between us.

I've never been so hot with need before. He's kissing me gently, but right now, I don't want gentle. I don't want tender. I just want *him*.

I'm filled with this well of desire, a deep, dark ache down low that throbs harder and harder by the second.

I thrust against him again, and he pushes back toward me. I moan at the feel of his hardness against me, hitting me right where I need him to. But I need him there with no clothes separating us.

I'm pinned to the couch, which makes it hard to back away to tell him, but I break our kiss and arch my neck. His lips trail along my skin.

"Now, Tristan. I need you now. I've waited too damn long to wait another second." My voice is hoarse and holds a certain desperation in it.

He pulls back, and I sit up a little, pulling my shirt over my head. For a second, I forget I'm pregnant—I forget how my stomach isn't smooth and flat anymore, but round with stretch lines along it.

He glances down at it and back at me, his eyes round, and I'm afraid I've killed the moment by simply taking off my shirt.

It's a cold bucket of water to my hot libido, but then he says the words that ignite the fire once more.

"Holy shit. You—this…wow. You're really fucking beautiful." He bends down and presses a soft kiss to my stomach, and my chest tightens as tears fill my eyes.

I think I love him even more now than I did back then.

He reaches around me to unhook my bra, helping me out of it and tossing it aside. Even my swollen breasts ache with need for him. He brushes against my nipple, and it tightens into a tight bud. He runs his tongue along the surface, and it sends a shot of desire right down my spine. I can't help it when I cry out for more.

He sucks it into his mouth, and he works the other one with his hand as he incites emotions inside me that I haven't felt in years.

I've been with other men, sure. But not like this.

He stands and pulls me up with him. He leads me over toward the bed. "I need to get a condom," he says. He unbuckles his belt and tosses it on the floor.

I twist my lips. "So I don't get pregnant?" I ask.

He chuckles. "Are you okay doing this without one?"

"If you are," I say carefully.

"I am." He nods, and I trust him enough to know he means we're both in the clear.

He gently sweeps me into his arms like I'm not carrying a watermelon in my stomach, and I giggle as he lays me down on the bed. He sinks to the bottom of the bed and pulls my shoes off first, and then my socks, and then my pants. He lowers my panties last, and then he kneels between my legs.

I shake my head, and he chuckles.

"I want that later," I say softly. "But right now, I need you. And you won, so you get to choose the position."

He picks up my hand and kisses each of my fingertips. "I defer to you. I want you to be comfortable."

I smile, and then I move so I'm on my knees. "Then lie down, Higgins."

His eyes turn all lusty at my command, and I find I like the power trip it gives me. I always liked when he issued the orders, but this way is fun, too.

I pull off his shoes and socks, and then I flick the button on his jeans. His eyes are hot on me as I work, and I thought I'd feel self-conscious parading around naked, but I don't. It's not in his words but in his eyes. I always thought my memory betrayed me, that he never *really* looked at me like he worships me, that it was all in my mind…but he does, and it's the most confidence boosting thing I've ever experienced.

I'm beautiful because he believes it to be true, and he makes me feel it.

I run my hand along the hard outline of his dick over his jeans, and then I yank on the bottoms to pull them down. He helps, pulling his boxers down with them, and then I toss them to the floor before I crawl up the bed. I sit over his thighs, running my hands from his chest down to his abs and finally over his rock-hard cock. He groans as I take him in my fist, and my mouth waters. I want to taste him, too, but the ache in my pussy persuades me in a different direction.

I move forward and line his cock up with me, and then I lower myself onto him.

We both groan at the feel of his body sliding into mine, and I close my eyes as I savor the feel of him inside of me for the first time in far too long. I open my eyes to find him watching me, and the way his face is filled with need is the hottest thing I've ever seen.

He grabs onto my hips and helps set the pace as I move up and down over him, my body primed and ready for him. I've been waiting for this for seven years, after all, and he's ready for me, too. His hands glide along my stomach and up to my breasts.

My instinct is to close my eyes and give into the feel of him, but I can't seem to stop watching him as his eyes drink me in, appreciating every move my body makes. His eyes settle onto mine, and one hand stays on my breast, massaging and tweaking, while the other trails down to work my clit.

I yelp as he hits the exact right spot, and I shift a little, causing him to groan, too.

I remember it being good. I don't remember it being *this* good.

I want it to last forever, but I know it won't. All good things must come to an end, but I push that thought away as I take in the pure bliss of this moment—the way his fresh, clean scent takes over my senses, the way his moans spur my movement so he'll make those sounds again, the way his face is screwed up with pleasure.

I sense a shift coming, the tide changing—the pleasure building. I lean forward, bracing myself with my palms on his shoulders. I tilt my head back and close my eyes as he keeps working my clit, and then something snaps in me as I ride him and he works all my most sensitive zones.

He can tell I'm there as he says his next words. "Come for me, baby."

Why are those words so freaking hot?

I cry out as my body tightens over his. the tightness must push him into his own climax because he yells out, too.

"Oh fuck, Tessa, yes!"

I echo his sentiments as my body contracts over and over on top of his, and he thrusts into me a little faster, working me from the bottom as we both hit the wall of bliss at the same time.

We're both panting as the throbs start to slow, the painful ache of waiting now replaced with a soft, warm glow. I don't want to move, don't want him to slip out of me, but I need to lie down.

After that, I'm spent.

It wasn't just the physical act of it, but the emotional one, too. It's the rush of being with somebody so familiar after all this time has passed—of being with the man I never thought I'd get to be with again.

It's real.

It happened.

It's love.

It's everything.

I shift, and I lie down beside him, my head on his chest and his arm around me. He strokes a pattern on my back with gentle fingertips, and I sigh in total contentment.

"I love you so much," he whispers. "I don't know what I did right to get you back in my life, but honestly, Tessa, I'm not sure I've ever been happier than I am this very second."

I press a kiss to his chest. "I love you, too. And I feel the same way."

He's officially free of his evil wife…now his *ex*-wife, and we're officially back together.

I went from being terrified I'd be raising a baby alone, or with my mother, to feeling like I have a partner.

It's crazy how quickly things have moved, but it was inevitable for us. We both had a hole in our lives only the other one could fill, and now we're finally getting our second chance.

I wish it could always be this blissful, this easy, that I could lie in his arms just like this and all the rest would fall away.

I wish I could ride in this calm forever, but I have a feeling the storm is already brewing.

CHAPTER 13

Tristan

I force myself out of bed for the sole reason that I want to take care of her. For as hot as it is to have a woman holding all the control as she moves naked on top of me, it has to be hard on the thighs no matter how in shape a woman is. And *this* particular woman is carrying an extra ten pounds right now that surely made it even harder.

I turn on the water in the large tub in our bathroom, and she walks up behind me a beat later. "Is that for you or me?" She runs her fingers along my spine before moving in to hug me from behind, and I turn to hold her naked body against mine.

"Both of us."

"Great idea," she murmurs, and she moves to rummage through her toiletry bag. She pulls out her shower gel, and I see it's the same jasmine scent I used to buy for her. The bottle has a different design but the name's the same. "Bubbles?"

"Always," I say with a nod, and she chuckles.

"How hot is the water?"

"You can turn it however you want it."

She tests it and turns it a little cooler. "If my body temperature rises more than two degrees, it's not safe for the baby," she explains as she squirts some of the shower gel into the tub. The room immediately fills with her scent.

There's so much I don't know. So much I want to learn. "I didn't know that. Is there anything else I should know?"

"Baths are incredible for pregnant women—relaxing, and they take the pressure off my stomach for a bit—but I can't stay in longer than ten minutes or so." She looks a little sad as she says it, and admittedly the thought of sitting in the tub with her for hours sounds like heaven, but being safe is more important.

"Perfect, because I have a plan that starts in eleven minutes."

She giggles. I don't have a plan, but I had to say something to wipe that sad look off her face.

I get in first, and I help her in second. She settles in between my legs, and my dick grows hard at having this gorgeous, naked, slippery wet woman in my arms. I lean forward to smell her hair, and I press a soft kiss to her neck. She sighs with content then leans back against me, and my dick prods into one of her ass cheeks.

She doesn't seem to mind.

In fact, she grinds her ass a little, goading me on.

My cock needs a break to recharge, though, so I lean back and rest my head on the back of the tub, lacing my arms around her and toying with her nipples.

"That's only going to lead us back to the bed," she practically moans.

"Exactly where I planned to lead you," I whisper as the fresh memory of what just happened between us washes over me.

It wasn't just the best sex of my life. It was filled with meaning for me.

It was that feeling of riding a bike, so to speak—in one way it was comforting as my body woke up with the realization that *we've been here before*, but it was also new and different. Better than before, if that was even possible—or maybe my memory betrayed me. She felt so tight and sweet as she moved over me, but my chest exploded with all these different emotions while we connected in the deepest way two people can connect.

I wash her gently with a washcloth since we don't have much time in here, and then she gets out to dry while I wash myself, too. It's quick, and there's no wine or candles, but it still feels like the most romantic bath I've ever taken.

"So what was the eleven minute plan?" she asks once we're both out of the tub.

She's put clothes back on—a simple maternity t-shirt and shorts—and I suppose I should do the same. I grab my basketball shorts and a pair of boxers, but I skip the shirt.

Her eyes zero in on my abs. "Have I mentioned that you're really freaking hot?" She steps over toward me, and she lets her fingertips glide along each muscle there. My dick perks up again in response to her touch.

"That's only going to lead us back to the bed," I say softly, repeating her own words back to her.

"Exactly where I planned to lead you," she says, repeating my response back to me.

I chuckle, and then I lean down to kiss her, which only leads to me lying her down on the bed, getting rid of our clothes, and slipping into her.

I stand over her this time, careful not to crush her or make her feel uncomfortable in any way, and I slide slowly in and out of her, taking my time as my hands wander along the soft ridges of her body. She warned me that her body was different, and she's right—it is. But something about the way her body looks now is even more beautiful to me than before. It forces a realization upon me that I love her exactly how she is, however that may be. I accept her and welcome her into my life any way I can get her.

I've never felt that way about anybody else.

It's nothing to do with looks at all. Savannah was one of the most beautiful women I've ever seen on the outside, but the evil lurking inside was a turn-off. And then there's the woman beneath me, the one I'm making love to as I take my time with her, slowly moving in and out of her tight body to the chorus of her soft moans as I feel her delicate skin, so soft after our bath together, the air filling with her jasmine scent, wrapping me up like a warm blanket.

She's beautiful on the inside, too. A light shines from her, a bright glow of selflessness as she gives her body over to the baby growing inside, a baby I already love with a ferocity that seems unimaginable to me.

But of course I do. She's one-half Tessa.

I feel the familiar fire ripping up my spine, but I force myself to calm down a beat. I don't want this to end. I've had sex over the last seven years, sure…but I've never made love to a woman. Not like I'm doing right now, as I ease slowly in and out, as our bodies rock together toward a climax. Her eyes open and fix on mine, and that's my undoing.

I tip my head back, my neck corded with the pressure of my release as I start to come, and she grabs onto my hands where they hold her hips, squeezing my hands tightly as she moans my name, her body tightening over me as she starts to come, too.

And then it's over much too soon. I lie beside her as I try to catch my breath, and I breathe in heavy gulps of her. She permeates my system like a drug I'm already addicted to.

I can't get enough, and I don't know if I ever will.

Honest **MISTAKE**

We must fall asleep, but I don't realize it until the rising sun wakes me. The light is peeking into our window already, and I wish I hadn't fallen asleep because all it did was take away time that we could've spent together.

At some point during the night, she moved to her side, and I moved in behind her. I sit up on my elbow, careful not to move her, and study her as she sleeps. She looks the same as she did back then. Her skin is smooth, but she has just the slightest new lines near her eyes and by her lips that tell me she's laughed and cried over the years we were apart.

I wish I could've been there for every one of those moments. I wish I could've held her hand in the hard times and laughed with her in the good ones.

A few freckles dot her nose, and I remember more of them in the summer when she got too much sun. Her hair is a little longer and a little lighter. Her lips are almost smiling, and I wonder what she's dreaming about.

Her chest rises and falls softly with sleep. She's still naked, as am I, and as I watch her peacefully rest, my dick starts to wake up until it's pressing into her backside.

I thrust my hips gently, and she stirs just the tiniest bit. I shift until my cock lines up with the crack of her ass, just a nice spot to rest, not to penetrate, although now that I think about it…

She must wake as I'm moving behind her because she pushes her ass back into me. I reach down and slide my dick between her legs, and she moans. I thrust gently, moving along her slit but not slipping inside, and the feel of her body around me is nearly enough to make me come.

She lets out a soft morning moan, and then she tilts forward a little and reaches down between us. She covers my cock with one hand so I'm sliding in between her hand and her slit, which seems to be growing hotter by the second.

And then she shifts and pushes me inside her. "Good morning," she murmurs.

Fuck yeah it is. What a way to wake up.

I grip onto her hip with one hand as I drive in slowly, lazily, and I lean down to kiss her neck. She shifts back, meeting me thrust for thrust, and despite having done this twice last night, I can't help when my body responds the way it does to her.

It's been too long.

Too long without sex. The last woman I was with was my ex-wife, and it's been a damn long time since we were together.

But that was just sex. This is different, and it's been far too long since I've felt these feelings. I never want it to stop.

CHAPTER 14

Tessa

We shower together, and he caresses every single inch of my body.

I've never felt so loved, so cherished, so important to anybody before. I think back to my last experience where Cam basically made me feel like a used piece of trash after the first time we had sex.

We all know how that ended up. I shake him out of my head. He deserves no real estate here, particularly not in this state of bliss where I find myself.

After we get dressed, we head down to the restaurant in the hotel for breakfast.

And that's when a little corner of our blissful night breaks off into reality.

I hear his name whispered as the hostess takes us back to our table. I see the not-so-stealthy aim of smartphones as they try to catch a covert image of the celebrity walking through the restaurant. The heat of his hand where it lies on the small of my back as he presses us toward our table feels like fire.

My brain is riddled with all the things people will see.

I'm not sure if his divorce is public yet, so people probably don't know he's no longer married.

His hand is on a pregnant woman in a hotel near his hometown early in the morning.

We both have wet hair.

It doesn't take a genius to figure out what's going on here.

"Are you Tristan Higgins?" a young boy with enough nerve asks him. He's maybe seven or eight, and my chest tightens as I think about *our* boy. He'd be around the same age. He'd have already lost his two front teeth, and big ones that look too big for his mouth would already be growing in—just like this boy.

What if this is him?

What if he's our boy?

Will I ever stop looking at boys around the right age and wondering if it's him?

I glance at his parents, and he looks just like his dad. It's probably not our boy…but still.

Tristan nods and smiles at the boy.

"Can I get a picture with you?" the boy asks.

"Of course," Tristan tells him, and his hand leaves my back so he can kneel down beside the boy.

I feel a rush of cold air without him beside me.

He talks to the boy and his parents a minute, and then he stands and we head toward our table. We're near the window at a regular sort of table. There are no tall booth walls to give us privacy, and I see the same not-so-covert smartphone angles already poised in our direction.

I hide behind a menu. "Is it always like this?" I ask softly. He's across the table from me—too far, but also far enough that the focus will be on him and not so much on his breakfast companion.

He sighs. "Yeah, pretty much. I guess I sort of forgot it might be new to you. My ex-wife preferred the spotlight, so I guess I just got used to going out and it not being a big deal."

"I, uh…I don't want people knowing who I am." I say the words softly so nobody overhears.

He clears his throat, and then he pushes down on the top of the menu I'm hiding behind so his eyes can meet mine. "Why not?"

"I just don't like the idea of people digging around." I glance down at my stomach then give him a meaningful look. "And, well…you know." It's not just the baby, though.

It's my entire history that I don't want people finding out about.

He nods his understanding. "I get it. We can talk more later, but I think I have a solution."

I hardly believe he has a solution to the issues he knows nothing about, but I nod and offer a small smile before my gaze returns back to the menu.

* * *

"Don't do this," he says quietly once we're back in the privacy of our hotel room.

"Don't do what?" I ask.

He sighs and walks over toward the window. "I feel you withdrawing, Tess. I know my life is in the spotlight, and that can be weird or strange or difficult. But that doesn't give you a ticket out. Not after what we shared last night and this morning."

"I don't want a ticket out," I admit. "But I also like my privacy."

"Then we tell people the baby is mine," he says, and clearly that's his solution. "People won't dig to find out the truth if there's nothing to find. My divorce is final now so it doesn't matter. And I haven't spoken with my lawyer, but last we talked, he was going to send the paperwork over to Dr. Foster to have him sign off on his rights."

"So let me get this straight. Your solution to my issue with people finding out who fathered my child is lying about this baby's paternity and making it appear to the general public that I'm a homewrecker?"

"No!" he says, shaking his head. "That's not at all what I'm saying. I'm saying I make a statement about how my marriage has been over for nearly two years. I doubt anyone would expect that I was living as a monk that whole time."

"But, according to you, you were."

He shrugs. "Yeah, I know. I was. I slipped up with Savannah a few times, but I never cheated on her."

"You're a better man than most," I say.

"Fuck lot of good it's gotten me," he mutters.

"People were snapping photos of us the entire time."

"I know." He blows out a frustrated breath. "I should've warned you that might happen."

"So what do we do when the headlines about the mystery woman start to appear?" I ask.

"If you don't want to say I'm that baby's father, then we tell them the truth."

"That we fucked twice last night and once this morning?" My brows dip.

"First of all, that was way more than a fuck, Tessa," he says thickly. "And second, that's not at all what I meant. We tell them we're old friends and we decided to catch up over breakfast."

"Fine." I start packing up my overnight bag. "Tell them that. We'll figure out the rest later."

"What are you doing?" he asks.

I shrug. "Don't we need to check out soon?"

He nods, and he looks sad about it. I feel sad about it, too.

I walk over to where he stands near the window, and I touch his shoulder. "Excluding breakfast, this has been the best date of my life. I don't want it to end. I don't want to leave, but we have to get back to reality. The festival is three days away, and I have a long list of things to do."

He pulls me into his arms, and it feels safe and warm here. I rest my head on his chest.

"I don't want to leave, either, but let's get out of here. Let's tackle that to do list together, and then we can slip back into our own version of reality."

I smile, but it feels a little half-hearted. It's not like we can just bang in my childhood bedroom with my mother asleep down the hall—or in his house, for that matter, because of the same reasons. I don't know what the future holds for us, but living in my mom's house doesn't feel like a good long-term plan.

Maybe it's time to start planning what comes next.

CHAPTER 15

Tessa

The next two days pass in a blur of lists and checkmarks.

I've barely had time to process that my photo is all over the internet alongside Tristan. I've set that aside. I can take a deep dive into it all and figure out where we go from here after the festival, but right now, that is taking all my focus.

I've double checked everything, made about a million calls verifying everyone is ready to go, and now it's just a waiting game. I'm loading up the back of my car with banners and tablecloths I've been storing in the garage to take downtown when Tristan walks out his parents' front door.

"Let me help," he says, and he grabs a few loads and carries them to the car for me.

"Mrs. Harrison said I can store these on the first level at the B and B until morning. I was just going to drop a load off so there's less to carry tomorrow," I say.

"You can use my truck if you've got more," he offers. "You need me to do anything else?"

"Maybe stop by the high school and just make sure Coach is all set getting the tables and chairs downtown?"

He nods. "Can I take you somewhere first?"

My brows knit together. "I don't have a lot of time for *that*," I tease.

He laughs. "Oh trust me, *that* is all I've been thinking about since our date."

"It's all I've been thinking about, too," I admit. "Once this festival is over, maybe life will get back to normal." I say the words out of some ingrained habit, but then I realize…I don't really have a normal. I don't even know what *normal* means right now.

I have a baby on the way. I have no plans for the future. I'm living with my mom, and my boyfriend who lives next door is leaving soon to go back home.

Maybe the better phrasing is that once the festival is over, I can start planning for the future.

"Normal's overrated." He winks, and then he gets into my passenger seat. I drive us downtown, and he empties my backseat and the back of the SUV, carrying it to Mrs. Harrison's first floor.

Once the car is empty, he grabs my hand. "Come with me."

We walk down the block, and he stops in front of Mr. and Mrs. Cunningham's corner house.

There's just something about that house.

I've been inside it a few times for different occasions—that one progressive dinner, or because my mom had to talk to Mrs. Cunningham about something, or when there was a Christmas cookie exchange Mrs. Cunningham hosted.

It's a dream of a house.

The balcony off the top floor overlooks the town I fell in love with as I fell in love with the boy next door, and the wraparound porch and the white picket fence makes it feel like something out of an actual fantasy. But the inside is what I always loved about it.

The floor plan was so beautiful to me. It's open and spacious, with the first room when you walk in being a beautiful living room with tall ceilings. A huge Christmas tree sat in the front window at Christmastime, a fire roaring in the fireplace in the same room, and the staircase to go up was both grand and impressive. The floors were hardwood, and from the front door you could see the dining room and into the kitchen, which, as I recall, was all sparkling white and gorgeous.

I'm not sure what it is about this house, but any time I need to call up an image of my dream home, for some reason…this is it. It's big but not a mansion at a little under four thousand square feet, with five spacious bedrooms and three full bathrooms plus a half bath.

There's a shed out back that would be a perfect *she shed*, or, if I was living here with Tristan as I always dreamed, a perfect spot for a home gym. And the backyard is chef's kiss perfection to raise children with plenty of grass to run around in and a fancy playground that was always the envy of all the kids in town.

He walks up the porch, tugging me along with him, and he unlocks the front door.

"What are you doing?" I whisper-yell. "You can't just walk in."

He laughs. "Why not?" He pulls me inside with him, shutting the door behind us.

And then he twirls me right there in the front room, dipping me down low and planting a kiss on my mouth.

When I come up for air, that's when I notice…there's no furniture in here.

The walls are empty, too.

As I recall, there was an entire row of framed photographs lining the stairwell, and they're just…not there now.

"What are we doing in here?" I ask, my voice muddled with confusion.

"I, uh…" He glances nervously at me, and then he takes a deep breath and nods as if he's strengthening his resolve.

My brows dip as I try to put together what the hell is going on.

"I bought it. For you. Well, for *us*, if you want me here."

"You…" The question forming in my head dies on my lips as I look around, and then I look back at him. His face is so…hopeful. So earnest. So loving. So…everything. "You bought it?"

He nods, a smile tipping up the corners of his lips as he gauges my reaction. "Yeah."

"I didn't know it was for sale," I say stupidly.

"It wasn't. But Mr. and Mrs. C were always going back and forth to Cedar Rapids, and they'd been debating selling the place but felt like it would be a big hassle. I made it a little easier for them."

"You bought it?" I say again.

He laughs. "For you, and the baby. And I'd love to live here with you, too, if you'll have me."

I feel a little dizzy.

I look around for somewhere to sit but come up empty since all the furniture is gone, and then I walk over to the stairs and sit on the bottom one.

"Are you okay?" he asks softly, slowly moving in my direction and standing over me.

I glance past him into the huge family room where I already see a Christmas tree in the front window and children laughing by the fireplace and Tristan's hand in mine on the loveseat as we look at our family. I see warmth and love and happiness…things I didn't think I was going to have in my life with him after what my father did to us. "I can't believe you did this."

"We can't stay in our parents' houses forever, and I know how much this town means to you, to me, to both of us. I'm not sure where you want to settle, and that's okay. It could just be a place for me if you don't want it, or if you don't like it, it wouldn't be hard to flip it and sell it, but you mentioned wanting a place for the baby and I know we're moving fast, but I want to be there with you for all of it. We need a home base because I don't know if I'll be in Vegas forever, and I thought…why not make Fallon Ridge our home base?" He's rambling, and his nerves over this whole thing might be the most adorable thing I've ever seen.

I stand, and I touch his arm to try to calm him. "I can't believe you did this for me. For us."

"I love you, Tessa. On the one hand, it feels fast, but on the other hand…it's been half our lives. You know?"

I nod, and I lean over to press a kiss to his cheek. "It's perfect. I don't know what to say. I don't know how to thank you. Nobody's ever bought me a house before." It sounds ridiculous saying it out loud. And it's not just any house. It's my dream house, and he knew that.

And now it's mine. *Ours.*

"You don't need to." He curls an arm around me and pulls me into him.

"I love you, and of course I want you here with me. I never want you to leave."

"I won't," he says. "I promise."

My heart squeezes and my chest aches.

He can't keep that promise. Not really.

Maybe he won't leave me in the emotional sense, but physically, we'll be apart. He mentioned he needs to go back for some workouts in April. April is just a week away, and then he'll leave me whether he wants to or not.

He holds me tightly against him, and then he backs up to angle his head down for a kiss.

His phone starts to ring, interrupting our kiss. "Sorry, I need to take this." He answers. "Tomorrow's not good, but Sunday or after works," he says. He says some more things as I start to walk around the house, imagining how I want to decorate it. It feels like way too big a space for my meager belongings. I need furniture. A couch. A dining table. A bed.

A crib.

I have a little bit of money saved from what Sara sold for me back in Chicago, but I was planning to use it to buy things for the baby.

He ends his call, and he turns to talk, but I beat him to it.

"Tristan, this is too much. I can't accept a *house* from you."

"It's already done. If you want, you can think of it as my house and I'm just extending the offer to have you move in with me. Does that make it any better?" he asks.

I think it over. "It does, actually."

"I've got a crew of painters coming by later today to give it a fresh coat. Just white—you can pick colors later if you want. I just wanted a clean palette for you to start with. The cleaning crew has already been through, and after the festival we can get whatever furniture you want on order. Or, if you want me to, I can take care of all of it." He ducks his head a little as he tries to catch my eye, like he senses that I'm overwhelmed by all of it.

"I'd love to make those sorts of decisions together," I say softly.

He nods and grabs my hand. "Come with me."

We walk together up the stairs, and he pauses outside the third door we pass. "I was thinking this could be the baby's room." He opens the door, and sunlight floods the room. It's cheerful even though it's empty. The room overlooks the backyard, and I get the sense a little girl would love growing up in here. I picture a four-poster bed with a big pink canopy—the exact bed I wanted when I was little.

"I figure it's the second closest room to the master bedroom so it's not too far for those late-night wake-up calls, but it's far enough away that any extracurricular noise won't wake her up." He winks at me, and I giggle even as tears form in my eyes.

"You've got it all figured out," I murmur, and he nods.

"I've been planning this a little while. I figured you'll never know if you don't ask, and Mr. and Mrs. C were incredible about the whole transaction," he says. "They were especially pleased that the legacy of the home they built forty years ago would go to a family who call this their hometown as well."

"A family," I repeat. Baby girl, me, and Tristan.

"If it's okay. If it's what you want."

I walk over to the window and overlook that perfect backyard. I picture rounds of hide-and-seek and hours pushing our children on the swing set and Adirondack chairs with a firepit in front of it and roasted marshmallows and glasses of wine and laughter. So much laughter. So much joy.

"I don't want you to think for a second that it isn't everything I've dreamed about since I was twelve," I admit. "But I want you to make sure you realize what you're getting into."

"I know exactly what I'm getting into, Tessa. And it's everything I've wanted since I was twelve, too. It's you, and that's all that matters to me. You are everything."

"I hope I can live up to the picture you have of me in your head," I say softly.

He walks over and stands behind me, wrapping his arms around my waist in a backward hug. "You already do. Every single day."

"Then I want you to stop saying things like *if it's what you want*. You are what I want. You, me, and our baby." I run my hand along my stomach, and he does the same, following my path. I place my hand over his, linking my fingers through his, and it's our silent vow that maybe he's not biologically this baby's father, but he'll be her daddy in every way that matters. It's the first time I've called her *ours*, and I want him to feel the power of those words as we both hold a hand over where she's growing.

    I turn in his arms and kiss him as we seal that vow. It's another moment I wish could last forever, another moment of calm that only signals to me that the storm is coming.

    I just didn't realize it would be coming quite so soon.

CHAPTER 16

Tristan

Something changed inside that house.

She finally saw how much I want this—how sincere I am in my words that I want to be with her, that I want a future with her. I guess I needed a pretty huge grand gesture to prove it, and showing her that I want her in my life long term in the form of a house seemed to be the thing that finally convinced her.

I know what I'm getting into, and I also know it's exactly where I want to be.

Her eyes lit up when I told her it was ours now, and I want to continue to do things that make her eyes light up in that way.

It was a beautiful break from the stress of planning the festival tomorrow. She's worked so hard, and on top of growing a life inside her, it's overwhelming. So to be able to take a minute to breathe inside our new home…it just meant a lot to both of us.

After we decided on the baby's room, we walked across to the master bedroom. We stepped out onto the balcony that's in pretty good shape but in need of some repairs. I made a mental note to have my dad double check it, but I'm pretty sure I'll be able to fix it myself.

We looked downtown. I've never been up on this balcony, but I can imagine taking a minute to watch the festival tomorrow from up here, or the Corn Boil later in the year, or the fireworks on the Fourth of July. It's a place where I imagine rocking chairs and a glass of whiskey as we overlook the town where we first fell in love.

She's letting me in. She's giving me the things I hoped she would, and I really feel in my heart that she's not doing it because she's scared to do it alone or because she's trying to fill some void. She's doing it because we were always meant to be together. It just took a little extra time to get it right.

I don't want to leave, but we have to get back to work. She needs to get back home, and I need to run over to the high school to check on Coach and see whether he needs help transporting the tables and chairs.

We stand on the front porch for a beat after I lock the front door, and we both stare at the door for a second. The house is white, and I've got a painter coming to freshen up the exterior, too.

"You like the red front door?" I ask.

She smiles softly as she stares at it. "I *love* the red front door." She glances over at me. "And I love you."

My eyes soften as I toss my arm around her shoulders and pull her into me. I press a soft kiss to her temple, and then I grab her hand and we head back toward my truck.

I drive slowly along the street because that's what you do in Fallon Ridge. The posted speed limit is twenty-five, but rarely does anyone go that fast…unless it's a teenager. They tend to drive double the speed limit, and they've been known to compete in drag races that start downtown and end up in the fields beyond the high school, though the local law enforcement does their best to put a stop to that.

"I was thinking about how I have no ideas for names for the baby," she says. "And I was wondering if you had any."

My chest tightens as the realization dawns on me. She wants me to be a father to the baby as much as I want to be.

"I always liked Emma and Madison," I say, but somehow those don't feel right.

"Those are lovely names," she says.

"What names do you like?" I ask. I pull onto the street behind ours.

"I don't know. I have a few I keep thinking about, but I haven't settled on anything."

"What are they?"

She clears her throat. "I like Violet and Riley, but my grandmother on my mom's side was Caroline, and I think that's a pretty name."

"Do you want a name with meaning?" I ask.

She lifts a shoulder. "It doesn't matter. When we were together, I always imagined a T name since we're T and T."

I chuckle. "What about Dynamite?"

She giggles. "Hi everyone, meet baby Dynamite! We call her Dyna for short."

"I love it," I joke. "What about Tori?"

She shrugs. "Definitely not Tiffany," she says as we pass Tiffany Gable's parents' house.

"What do you have against Tiff?" I tease, though the teasing feels misplaced given the fact that I have a few things to hold against her myself.

"She never hid the fact that she wanted you even though you were with me," she points out.

"But I wanted *you*, so it never mattered." I reach over and squeeze her hand. "You were the only one I saw. The only one I cared about."

"You married someone else," she points out.

"A drunken mistake that took me two years to fix, but it's fixed now. And for the record, I never felt so much as an ounce for her compared to what I feel for you." I wish I knew a way to convince her how much truth is in those words.

I pull around the corner so we're on Oak Tree Lane, and I spot it immediately.

A white BMW sitting in my parents' driveway.

My heart sinks.

I thought this was over. I thought we were done.

She's never been here before, and I can't see any reason why she'd be here now.

"Who's car is that?" Tessa asks absently as we stop in front of my house and I put the truck in park.

I close my eyes when I see her standing by the front door.

I should have known she wouldn't just walk away easily.

"Savannah," I hiss.

CHAPTER 17

Tristan

I leap out of the truck as my body seemingly prepares for battle.

My chest tightens, my jaw is set, and my eyes harden. My armor is on, and I will do whatever it takes to protect the woman I love from the woman I…don't love.

"What the fuck are you doing here?" I hiss, and I feel Tessa's presence as she moves in behind me.

"Is this the one that's been causing all the problems?" Savannah asks, looking just over my shoulder.

"No. You are the one who caused all the problems," I say.

Savannah shakes her head with a bit of disgust. "You didn't push for the divorce until you came back to this hellhole of a town, and suddenly it's old times again for the two of you?" She rolls her eyes. "Listen, Tris. You know I've been doing my due diligence, and I came to tell you the truth about her."

I hold up a hand. "That's enough, Savannah. I know everything I need to know, and last I checked, our divorce is final and I'm through with you. You can see yourself out of this *hellhole* of a town." I turn to walk down the driveway, grabbing Tessa's hand on the way so I can walk her home.

"Can we just talk for two minutes?" she asks. "Alone?"

Tessa squeezes my hand, and I can't tell if she's clutching me closer in solidarity or if it's more her way of telling me not to do it.

Either way, I make my own decisions. "No," I tell Savannah. "You can take your last-ditch effort to get me back and shove it."

"That's not why I'm here," she says. "You know I've always just wanted what was best for you, and this?" She nods toward Tessa. "This ain't it."

I spin around to face her again. "You don't know what the fuck you're talking about. Leave. Get out of Fallon Ridge. Get out of Vegas. Get out of my life." I hear the fatigue in my own voice, but frankly I'm tired of going round after round with her. "I don't want you here. Nobody does, and it's over, Savannah. *We* are over. Move on. Find someone else you can make miserable because it can't be me anymore."

We're walking up Tessa's driveway when Savannah sighs loudly. "I'm not leaving. I'm here to attend the festival tomorrow. I've got a gaudy room at that hideous bed and breakfast in town, so I'll be close."

Tessa's unlocking her front door while Savannah's talking, and I walk in behind her and slam the door shut.

"Fuck," I say, and then I yell, "Fuck!" as I punch a balled up fist into my other palm.

Tessa wraps her arms around me, and it's the calm I need with my ex-wife slithering around town. I stand there a beat as I allow her comfort to wash over me, and then I loop an arm around her waist.

"God, I hate her," I say.

"Why is she doing this to you?" she asks.

"That's a great question. I don't really know." All I know is that she fixates on things to the point of obsession, and when Luke warned me of that when we first got together, I ignored him. I never thought it would actually turn dangerous. I never thought the fact that she digs into people's history was a sign of anything other than her doing her job.

But maybe it's something bigger than that.

"I keep trying to figure out the meaning behind all of it—why she so badly wants to be married to a football player, why she sinks her claws in and doesn't let go. All I can think is that she's driven everyone she ever loved away because of her behavior, and now she's lonely."

"Have you met her family?" she asks, pulling out of our hug and walking over to the kitchen table.

I shake my head as I follow her. "She and her mother have been estranged since her parents got divorced when she was a freshman in high school. She chose to live with her father, but from everything I've ever heard about him, it sounds like he was pretty emotionally unavailable. He died on her twenty-third birthday."

"Why'd she choose to live with him if he was emotionally unavailable?" She sits, and I take my seat beside her.

I shrug. "She didn't talk about it much, but I got the sense her mother was involved with other men who possibly didn't treat Savannah very nicely."

Tessa's brows dip. "That's really sad, but I think you just summed up her attachment issues, Tristan. Was her father a football fan?"

"I think so, yes." I nod. "I remember her telling me how much he loved Jack Dalton when they were together, but Jack broke up with her."

"There you go. And she was married before?"

"She ended up marrying Jack's brother, Luke. She blackmailed him, too. It's just the way she is." I sigh. I really, really, *really* wish I would've listened to Luke when he tried to warn me off her. Everything he said was the truth—including that she'd blind me with sex and promises only to bail on all of it the second she roped me into marriage.

God, I was stupid. I wasted so much time on her.

I'm not sure how much it *really* matters, though, in the long run. Tessa wasn't in my life for the majority of my time with Savannah, and all it took to push me in the right direction was the mere thought of getting her back.

But I should've known she wouldn't just lie back and take it. She spent two years fighting to stay married to me. She's not going to walk away quietly.

"She's just doing what she thinks her father would have wanted her to do, and now he's not here to tell her otherwise," she says quietly. "But if he was emotionally unavailable, he might not have tried to guide her in a different direction anyway."

I can't help but wonder if she's projecting her own insecurities on my ex-wife. "Are you?" I ask.

"What?"

"Doing what you think your father would have wanted you to do?"

She glances at me thoughtfully for a beat before she answers. "No. I hated my father for a long time, and there were things he did that I never forgave him for. And then he died, and I found out he was even worse than what I thought. It's not his approval I care about." She shakes her head. "I wish I had it in me to forgive him, though. It's like a big weight I'm carrying around, and I don't like the stress of it. But how do you grant forgiveness to somebody who's gone?"

"I don't know," I murmur. "I guess you just…do it. You let it go. Drop that weight so it stops holding you back."

"Tristan, I—" she begins at the same time I say, "I should go—"

She offers an awkward chuckle. "You go."

Honest **MISTAKE**

"I should go check on Coach and the tables and chairs," I say, wondering what she was about to say. "Will you be okay?"

"I'm fine," she says, and I gaze at her a beat to make sure I believe her words.

I press a kiss to my hand and lay it over her stomach, and then I lean in and brush my lips across hers.

She lets out a soft, contented moan, and then I push back from the table.

"I'll report back in a bit," I say, and she nods.

"Thanks for all you're doing," she says softly.

"Anything for you." I wink, but honestly I'm not sure I've ever meant anything more in my life. After running into Savannah, I realize I will do literally anything for Tessa.

Anything…even heading over to Mrs. Harrison's B and B to confront my ex-wife.

CHAPTER 18

Tessa

I sigh as I open the front door.

Part of me wants to tell her to freaking just get lost, and the other part of me is actually starting to get used to these drop ins. Maybe I should just sit her down and have a talk. Maybe we can actually move past this as sisters.

I mean, I doubt it, but I guess stranger things have happened.

"Tomorrow's the big day!" Stephanie squeals as she steps into my house uninvited. "What can I do to help?"

"It's all done, but thank you so much for stopping by," I say. "I was just going to lie down for a bit. I'm exhausted after working all morning."

"Oh, okay. I got a room at the bed and breakfast in town, so I'll be around. I'm so excited for the fair tomorrow! I spoke with Mrs. Burton when I was walking into the diner for lunch and she needs an assistant, so I'll be at her table all day tomorrow. Unless you need me to do anything, of course."

Is this chick high?

What the hell is she talking about?

Maybe I have pregnancy brain or whatever it is. My head feels a little foggy, and I just fended off one crazy lady only to have another show up on my doorstep.

I need a break from all this. I just want to go back to the house on the corner—*our* house—and sit on the stairs and stare into the family room and imagine a time when our lives aren't quite so tumultuous.

But today clearly isn't the day I get to do that.

"You…you're assisting Mrs. Burton?" I repeat.

She nods. "Right, but I told her I might need to help you out. She's so sweet, and her quilts are just gorgeous, right? I might take one or two home myself. A little Fallon Ridge souvenir. I might even replace the pinecone on my end table I picked up when I walked through the park last time."

I let the strangeness of that one slide as I think about Tristan's words to me. *She's got some of the same traits Savannah has and it's both toxic and scary.*

He's right, and the more I get to know about each woman, the more parallels I see.

They're both searching for their father's approval but can no longer get it.

They both appear as if from out of nowhere.

They both have personalities bordering on obsession.

They both seem to have addictive traits.

I don't know a ton about psychology, but I took a few classes in my pursuit of my nursing degree.

There's something off about both of them, and now they're staying at the same bed and breakfast—the only place in town with rooms to rent. I imagine they'll run into each other at some point if they haven't already, and the thought of them teaming up together is, frankly, terrifying…but also one hundred percent realistic.

For whatever reason, they seem to want the same thing, which is Tristan and me apart.

I'm scared that not one but *two* women are already trying to come between the two of us when we've barely even gotten back together. We haven't even identified what we are yet, although he bought me a house. That seems to put us decidedly in the *serious* category.

Still, I can't imagine how many countless others there will be hoping to tear us apart given Tristan's status.

I brush away the thought for now and focus on what's in front of me. "Thanks for the offer, but I think we're all set. I'm sorry to cut this short, but I really need to go lie down." I hold my stomach a little dramatically for effect, and her eyes widen.

"Is everything okay?" she asks.

"Yes, everything's fine. I'm just exhausted." I offer a tight smile as I walk over toward the door, expecting her to do the same.

"You're twenty-six weeks along?" she asks instead.

I nod. "Yep."

She offers a smile and winks at me. "Good to know, you know, just in case."

"Always good to be prepared," I say weakly. "I'm sorry, but I'm going to have to ask you to leave. I'll see you tomorrow."

She looks mildly offended that I'm kicking her out, but I really don't want her standing over me petting my hair while I'm trying to take a twenty-minute power nap—something I desperately need right now.

It's been a day.

A good day, but still, a day. Good stress is still stress, and the thought of moving out of my mother's house and with Tristan into the house on the corner gives me a new type of butterflies I didn't know existed. Even back when we were together in high school, I figured we'd stay together, but actually moving in together was a thought so far into the future that it never really seemed like a reality.

And now, he bought me a freaking house.

And not just any freaking house. *The house on the corner.*

It's thrilling and scary and comforting and right all at once, and I'm starting to think that maybe the best things in life are a combination of all those things.

I lie down and close my eyes, but I don't fall asleep. I hear my bedroom door open a short while later, and I open my eyes. It's my mom.

"Come on in," I say, and I sit up and lean against the headboard. "Can we talk a minute?"

She nods, a look of concern coloring her eyes. "Is everything okay?"

I nod. "Sorry for worrying you. Everything's fine." I smile, and I can't help when the smile seems to stretch on forever. "It's wonderful, actually. I have some news."

She looks at me hopefully as she sits on the edge of my bed and takes my hand between both of hers.

"Tristan and I are back together," I say. "Officially."

She lets out a soft gasp. "Oh, honey. That's wonderful. Have you told him about—"

I cut her off with the shake of my head, and she nods.

"He told me he just wants to focus forward," I say. "To focus on the baby. *Our* baby."

"*Our*…but what about the father?" she asks.

I sigh. "You know he wanted nothing to do with her. Tristan had his lawyer send over some papers to make sure it's all legal. Tristan said he wants to raise her with me."

"He wants to be her father?" she asks, a touch of incredulity in her tone.

I nod. "We haven't discussed it yet, but I think I might list him as the father on the birth certificate."

"Can you do that?" she asks.

I lift a shoulder. "I need to look into it, maybe ask Tristan's lawyer."

"That's a good idea. I just…" She trails off as she searches for the words. "It's a lot. Does he realize what he's getting into? Do *you*?"

"Does any first-time parent?" I counter.

She chuckles and shakes her head. "Good point."

"We want to be together. We want the same things. We want a family together, a family that should have started seven years ago." My voice breaks a little. "But we can start fresh now, and there's nobody who can take that away from us."

"Aren't you afraid he'll find out about…you know…?" she asks.

"I'll tell him someday. When the time is right. But now's not it. He bought me a house, Mama."

Her eyes grow round. "He bought you a *house*?"

I nod.

"Where?"

"Mr. and Mrs. Cunningham's house on the corner."

She gasps again. "Oh, Tessi-cat." Her eyes fill with tears. "Your dream house."

I nod. "He knew. He's always known. He asked, and they said yes. It's ours now."

"So you're moving out, but you're not moving far," she muses, squeezing my hand. "You'll be sticking around?"

"It looks like we'll be sticking around in the off-season, anyway," I say, my lips lifting in a smile. "I only stayed away from this town out of fear of running into him. Well, that and the whole, you know, not wanting to be around Dad after what he did to me."

She nods. "I know." She brushes away a tear. "I'm just so happy you'll be here, and I'll get to be close to help with my grandbaby."

I lean forward and toss my arms around her shoulders. "Love you, Mama."

She reaches up to pat my arm. "Love you, too, baby girl."

A family, a baby, a home, and Tristan. It looks like I will have everything I could ever want, and it's all coming together where we started in Fallon Ridge.

I just wish I could get rid of the feeling that something is going to tear it all apart before it becomes our reality.

CHAPTER 19

Tristan

She did an incredible job. I take a minute to walk down Main Street, admiring all the things we talked about as they came to fruition because of Tessa's incessant work.

How do you thank someone for taking an idea you had in your head and making the entire thing come to life?

The set-up is just about complete. The vendors are all in their booths, volunteers are in place, and crafters are setting out their products to sell today. I see the bounce houses across Main Street near the park, and behind me I see the huge "beer garden" the Fallon Tavern put out with barricades in front of their restaurant. The street is closed with traffic rerouted on the frontage road around town, the deejay is already pumping music down the boulevard, and the weather is perfect at a brisk fifty-nine degrees. With the sun shining, it feels warmer than that, but a calm and cool breeze keeps any of us from overheating.

All in all, it's perfect. We're ready to go.

I see my girl walking down the other side of the street as she checks in with each of the crafters to ensure everyone has everything they need. Her hand is on her belly as she smiles at whatever Mrs. Sullivan is saying to her, and a swell of love rushes through my chest.

"What are you staring at, motha-fucka?"

I jump at the sound of Travis's voice behind me, but I turn and grin as I see my buddies walking toward me.

They look beyond out of place here.

A lean wide receiver, golden tan from whatever vacation he just came back from. A bulky cornerback with chocolate skin who looks too big for our tiny, cobblestoned streets. A tight end who stands taller than the rest of the group, another wide receiver with lighter hair and lighter eyes than the rest. And a retired wide receiver who I'm frankly surprised to see here today—with his wife, my publicist, on his arm.

Travis, Patrick, Austin, Cory, and Luke.

Five guys who are salt of the Earth kind of people, men I can rely on, men who are more than just teammates. Men who are friends, men with whom I share a bond that will last forever.

I nod over toward Tessa. "My girl."

Travis's eyes dart over toward the girl in question, and they widen when he sees her pregnant belly. "Whoa. You made quick work of that." He moves in for a handshake and a one-armed hug where he pounds me on the back, and I do the same back to him.

I shrug, leaving out the details by not saying anything at all. I glance at Ellie, who's jaw is slightly dropped open as her brows knit together.

"She's gorgeous," Ellie says instead of asking the question I know she wants to ask. I'm sure her publicist brain is working overtime at how we're going to explain this one, but it's all fine. The baby is mine. That's all anybody needs to know. How she became mine and whether we're related by blood is nobody's business but ours.

"So does this mean no more Thursday night crew?" Austin asks, giving me the same handshake-hug Travis did.

Honest MISTAKE

I laugh at the sheer look of disappointment on his face. "I will always have a place for my Thursday night crew."

"Jaxon and Deon send their apologies they couldn't make it," Patrick says, coming in next. "Both are out of town."

"No worries," I say, and Patrick and I grab hands in a half handshake, half high-five as we bring it in for another one-armed hug. "I'm glad you assholes made it."

Cory's next, then Luke, and I give Ellie a regular hug last.

"Thank you all for coming. Now get your asses to the volunteer tent and get your assignments," I joke, and they all laugh.

"You're not giving us the special treatment?" Cory asks.

"Happy to," I say with a nod, and I lead them over to Tessa.

Her jaw drops open when she sees who's with me. "Oh my God," she murmurs. "You said you'd get some Aces players to come by, but this is…this is…"

I clear my throat as her eyes zero in on Luke. Yeah, yeah, yeah. He's good looking. Women love him.

He's also happily married and he has kids.

"I know. He's not even a player anymore." I roll my eyes. "I swear I didn't invite him."

Luke and Ellie both laugh, and Ellie speaks up first. "I hope you don't mind that we crashed your event with these other guys. I'm Ellie, Tristan's publicist." She sticks out her hand, and Tessa shakes it, and something about the contact between the women feels monumental. It's my two worlds colliding together—two worlds I never thought had the ability to collide together, and yet it's happening.

It feels big. Important.

"Oh, so nice to meet you!" Tessa says, pulling Ellie in for a hug. "Thank you so much for all you did to help us with this festival."

"What can I do to help?" she asks, ignoring the fact that Tessa is pregnant…for now, anyway.

Tessa looks around, takes a deep breath as she pulls herself together, then starts firing off directives, and suddenly everyone is moving in different directions. She pairs everyone off so Ellie and Luke are volunteering in the beer garden first, Patrick and Cory are in the dunk tank, and Austin and Travis are hanging by the auction tables to push higher bids and interest. They'll rotate throughout the day, and I'll be there to check on everybody, too.

The gates are set to officially open in two minutes, and I swing by the beer garden first to make sure Ellie and Luke are okay.

"Everything okay over here?" I ask.

They both nod. "This will be fun," Luke says, holding up a plastic cup of beer he already got for himself.

Ellie rolls her eyes and jabs a finger toward her husband. "For him. I'll be busy taking photos to post to your social media. I also had Leah set up a site to collect additional donations. We'll push that with each post, and it'll close tonight."

"You are amazing," I say.

"Isn't she?" Luke asks.

She shrugs good-naturedly and leans in. "Now tell me more about Tessa. Is this serious between you two?"

I'm about to answer when I hear Ellie murmur darkly, "What the hell is she doing here?"

I turn my gaze in the direction she's looking, but I don't need to see who it is to guess who she's talking about.

"Some desperate attempt to get me back, I think," I murmur back.

Ellie sighs. "It's like no matter where we go, we can't escape my husband's exes."

Luke grins sardonically and holds up his beer. "Need one?"

"Maybe something stronger than that," I say.

Savannah spots me and crosses the street to us. "Well would you look at this? Both my ex-husbands in one place. You two should start a club."

"We did," Luke says with a sneer. "We call it the gratitude club and we each give thanks every day that we finally got you to sign those papers."

I can't help a snort-laugh at that. Our split is fresh and new, but there's a whole lot of truth to what he just said. "What are you doing here, Savannah?" I ask, cutting to the chase.

"Just checking out this amazing fundraiser you and your little girlfriend put together. I was thinking of doing a piece on foundations of current players and thought this might be a great place to start my research," she lies.

I only say *she lies* because I know her well enough to know she's spouting pure bullshit.

She's either here to spy on me or to intimidate Tessa. She's here in some desperate attempt to win me back, maybe. She's here for some reason she's choosing not to disclose, and I don't like a single thing about that.

"I'd be happy to fill you in on the foundation along with several other players and their foundations when we're back in Vegas," Ellie offers. "Feel free to make an appointment with my secretary."

"I'll just do my own research, thanks," Savannah says without bothering to even look at Ellie. Her eyes are on Tessa, actually, and it makes my skin crawl.

I take a step closer to Savannah so she knows that I know exactly where she's looking.

"Stay the fuck away from her," I murmur.

"Or what?" she asks, and she reminds me of a toddler throwing a tantrum for attention. She'll do anything to get the attention of whoever she wants, and she doesn't seem to care whether it's positive or negative attention.

I don't have an answer, but just as I open my mouth to spout something out, a gust of wind blows through, knocking down half of Mrs. Beatty's display of knitted caps. I bolt over to help her, leaving Savannah behind even though I'm sure it's a mistake.

It wasn't just Mrs. Beatty's display that was knocked over. A few other booths need help setting back up, and we find some extra clips to keep everything clamped down. I search around for Tessa, but the event has officially started and people are starting to mill around.

I get a weird feeling in my stomach that Savannah is up to something, and I don't like it at all.

I just need to find Tessa to warn her.

CHAPTER 20

Tessa

"I know about the baby," Savannah says behind me.

I stop walking and glance down at my stomach. I mean...it's pretty obvious at this point. "I'm sorry?" I say, turning around to face her as I try to figure out what she's talking about.

"The baby," she repeats. "I know about it."

"Can we chat a little later?" I ask, glancing down at my clipboard. Everything seems to be going pretty smoothly, but I need to move some volunteers around and check in to be sure nobody needs anything.

And water. I could really use some water. And a bathroom. Baby girl decided today's a good day to use my bladder as her personal trampoline.

"Right. I'm pregnant." I run a hand along my belly and leave it there a few beats.

"Yeah, no shit. I mean, I know about *this* baby, and who the father *really* is, too...but that's not the baby I'm talking about."

"Is there something I can help you with?" I ask, tilting my head as I brush off her words like she didn't just incite terror in my chest that's starting to seep into my veins.

She nods. "I think we need to talk."

"Now's not exactly a good time." I look around at the festival. Nobody knows what we're talking about even though plenty of people are walking past us, but I have a lot to do today.

"Then when?" she demands.

I don't exactly want this on my mind, and especially not today when I need to focus on helping raise money for a needy family in the community. I don't want to worry about what the hell this incredibly volatile woman is up to.

I sigh as I buckle. "Fine. Talk."

"I dug into your history and learned the real reason why you left Fallon Ridge your senior year. If you want to keep secrets, you should really cover your tracks a little better." She rolls her eyes.

"I left because my dad made me. I left because there was a good program at the school near my aunt to prepare me for my nursing degree." I repeat the same lie I've always told even though I know it won't be enough for her.

"You left because you were pregnant," she hisses. "Was it Tristan's? That's the only piece of the puzzle I can't confirm, although I'm willing to put money on the fact that the seventeen-year-old daughter of the town pastor wasn't sleeping around on her future NFL star boyfriend."

"I don't know what you think you found, but you're wrong," I say. I don't look at her when I lie. She seems too intent on ruining my life, and the tiniest slip-up will give her everything she needs to destroy me.

She cackles. "I'm not wrong about this."

I blow out a breath. "Yes, you are. You have no idea what you're talking about. What exactly do you want?"

"I want Tristan." Her words are simple and direct.

"Why? He doesn't love you."

"He did once," she said. "There's a reason two people get married, you know. It's not like I forced him into it."

"No, but you forced him to stay married to you. Would that have made your parents proud?" I don't know why I issue the jab—why I poke at an already angry woman—but it's out of my mouth before I can stop it.

She looks momentarily taken aback, like I knocked the wind out of her a little, but she simply purses her lips. "I *will* get him back."

"Why?" I whisper. "Why are you doing this?"

"Because I love him, too. You had your chance, and you blew it."

Rage swims in my blood. She has no idea what the hell she's talking about, and there's no way in hell she feels the same way about him that I do. She doesn't even know what love is. She's obsessed with him, obsessed with a certain lifestyle, obsessed with money and football and fame.

But she does *not* love him.

"So did you!" I practically yell at her, my clipboard rising above my head as I toss my hands into the air still clutching onto it.

"Whoa, whoa, whoa, ladies," a voice from below says, and I gasp as Luke Dalton comes to break up what's about to turn into a fist fight between a thirty-something divorcee and a pregnant twenty-five-year-old over the same man. Did he hear what she said? Will he tell Tristan? Will *she* tell Tristan? "As much as I'd love to watch Tessa kick your ass," he says to Savannah, "let's save the fight for after the fest, okay?"

I give him a grateful look, and the way he nods paired with his words tells me he's on my side.

"I'm sure you have things to take care of," he says to me. "As much as it pains me, I'll keep an eye on my ex-wife." He emphasizes the word *ex*.

"Thanks, Luke," I say as I walk by him on my way toward the volunteer tent.

I try to shake off that encounter as I walk through the festival. People are laughing and having a great time all around me. Fallon Ridge is getting a ton of business, the crafters are selling their goods, and we're raising all sorts of money for Landon's family.

This is it. The thing we've worked so hard for. I look around and see all the time and effort we've given to this over the few weeks.

It's incredible. It's overwhelming. And I wish I could enjoy it.

Instead, I'm wondering whether I should admit the truth to Tristan before she gets to him. He said he didn't want to know what happened back then, that he wants to focus forward on the future, and he's already told Savannah he doesn't want to hear what she has on me and my history.

Still, though, I can't help but fear how long it'll be before Savannah causes my entire world to come crashing down around me.

CHAPTER 21

Tessa

My arms are folded across my chest as I stare at two women seemingly having a pleasant conversation.

My chest tightens and my heart races as I glance over at the dunk tank, where Luke Dalton is currently sitting on a platform and his wife is tossing beanbags at the lever that will get him to fall.

He had to switch stations, which meant he had to take his focus off keeping Savannah at bay.

And now she's talking to my half-sister, the same half-sister who shares a common goal with her, and fear permeates my entire being from the top of my head to the tips of my toes.

They're smiling, and Stephanie is nodding while Savannah talks. Then Savannah smiles while Stephanie says something.

"Can I steal you away for a second?"

I jump, startled at the sound of a deep, raspy voice close to my ear.

"What are you looking at?" Tristan asks, and he follows my gaze over to his ex-wife and my half-sister. "Oh," he murmurs.

"It's fine. We're fine. Everything's fine," I say in some attempt to stop him from going over to talk to Savannah. My best bet is to just keep them away from each other.

"What do you think those two are up to?" he asks.

I shake my head as I purse my lips. "No idea," I murmur. "But they seem to share a common goal. Neither of them wants us together."

We watch as Tiffany Gable joins in on their conversation. My chest feels tight.

He nods before he slings an arm around my shoulders. "They can try their hardest, but they're not going to keep us apart. We're stronger than that."

I glance over at him, and his expression is so resolute, so *sure*, that I can't even dig up an argument to his words.

I need to tell him.

Not today, obviously, but he deserves to know at some point. He probably wouldn't even believe Savannah if she did tell him, so I'm not sure why I let her get to me.

I draw in a deep breath filled with his scent, and it instantly calms me. "I need to pee," I announce, and Tristan laughs. "Baby girl is bouncing on my bladder today."

"I assume you don't want to use the Porta-John?" he asks.

I laugh. "I was going to sneak into the Pizza Joint."

"I can do you one better," he says, and he grabs my hand and turns me around. We walk down the block and he pulls his keys out of his pocket, and then we walk up the steps of the corner house. *Our* house.

It still doesn't feel real. I don't know if it ever will, even after we move in and bring home our baby and celebrate holidays and actually live here.

"A nice, clean, *private* bathroom just for you," he says, and I run through the house to the first-floor bathroom.

After I finish my business, I head back out and find Tristan sitting on the bottom stair, his eyes on his phone.

"Where were you going to steal me away to?" I ask, and he clicks his phone off and slides it into his pocket.

"Here," he admits, holding his hand out with a dramatic flourish. "I wanted to give you a short break." He nods over to the camping chair set up in the family room. "I brought you a chair if you need to sit and there's some bottled water in the fridge. Do you need anything?"

I hold my hand out to help him to a stand, and as soon as he's up on his feet, I wrap my arms around him. "Thank you," I murmur softly into his chest as his arms come around me, too.

"I did have an ulterior motive," he admits.

I lean back and raise a brow. "Oh?"

He leans down to brush his lips across mine. "I've been thinking about that huge island in the kitchen and how gorgeous you would look spread out naked on it. Or bent over it. If we close the kitchen blinds, nobody would see anything…"

Heat pools between my legs at the mere thought of it.

I need to get back to the festival.

I need to check on everyone, make sure nobody needs anything.

He presses his lips more firmly against mine, and his hand drags slowly up my torso.

Screw it.

Everyone's fine. A ten minute break won't matter.

I let him guide me toward the kitchen with his hand on my lower back.

"We'll be quick," he says. "I know you need to get back, but I *will* take my time with you on this counter. On another day, when we have more time, I will lick my way through your sweet pussy and I will enjoy every single second of it."

He tugs at my jeans, and I frantically pull them down my legs with my panties, eager for him and for this moment and for everything he's saying.

"But today, I want you to bend over. I need to feel you. Your body. I need to know this is real, that *you* are real. That this is all really happening and it isn't just some dream where you give up nearly two months of your life to plan the first event for our foundation together. I want to make this a tradition for every event we attend together where we find a way to sneak off to be together even if it's just for a few minutes."

"Oh," I moan softly as he slides a finger into me from behind as he finishes talking.

"Jesus, that's wet," he murmurs, and then I hear him rustle around a little as he unzips his jeans, too. "You're ready for me."

"I'm always wet for you," I say, my voice rising as he plunges into me while I talk. "Oh, yes," I murmur as I feel his cock slide in and out of me.

"I'm always hard for you," he grunts, and he slides forward again.

"Harder," I say, and he answers with a more ferocious drive. He picks up the pace, too, moving harder and faster, and then he leans over me and uses his fingers to rub my clit in fast circles.

The feelings I have for him seem to inexplicably deepen as we connect in this way, and I lose all sanity and control as he completely owns my body.

"Oh fuck, Tessa," he growls, and his words paired with the feel of him rocking into me push me over the edge. He hits his release at the same time, slowing his thrusts and pushing harder into me a few more times as his grip on my hips tightens and the sound of his groans fills the room.

He pulls out of me and spins me around, and then his mouth finds mine, his kisses hot and frenzied as we both attempt to come back down after that.

He pulls back and leans his forehead to mine. "I love you," he murmurs.

"I love you, too," I whisper back.

I just hope love is enough for whatever the outside forces are plotting against us…because I'm not ready to stop living in this fantasy with him.

CHAPTER 22

Tristan

"It's yours?" Travis asks. His voice is quiet as we walk from the beer tent to the auction table. Austin decided to *volunteer* in the beer garden a little longer as he chats with Tiffany Gable. I gave him a warning look, but he ignored me in much the same way I ignored Luke when he warned me about Savannah.

Travis is the one guy I can level with. The one guy I trust not to tell anyone if I tell him the truth. He's my best friend, and apart from my parents, I've been making these decisions and going through this virtually alone.

I don't need anybody except Tessa.

That still holds true. I haven't *felt* alone because I have her. And yet…somehow having a friend reaching out feels like what I need anyway.

"In all the ways that matter, she will be," I finally answer.

"That's sort of what I figured. So Tessa's your ex?" he asks.

I nod. "I guess you can call it that, although technically we never broke up. It was our senior year of high school, and one day over spring break she just vanished."

"Vanished?" His brows furrow.

I nod. "Her dad sent her off to Chicago to finish high school and live with her aunt."

"Why would he do that?" The furrow deepens.

I shrug. "He was a pastor, a man of God, and I guess he didn't like that his daughter was engaging in sinful acts with the boy next door. So he removed the temptation."

He frowns a little. "I feel like it doesn't add up, man."

"You know what? It doesn't to me, either, but I also feel like it doesn't matter. She's back now. We're together again. She's pregnant, and I'm fucking *finally* divorced. We both made mistakes." I leave it at that.

"Why aren't you pushing for the truth? If I was in your shoes, I sure as fuck would be."

I glance back at Austin, who's saying something to Tiffany. She throws her head back and cackles. "Maybe we both have things that are better left in the past," I murmur.

He nods, and then we're at the auction table. "Oh, come on. Jaxon Bryant's signed football has a higher bid than my jersey?" he jokes to someone checking out the items, and he garners himself another bid.

I chat with the locals, too, who all have similar questions about my life in the league. It's fun answering them with my best friend beside me. He's entertaining and hilarious, and all the older ladies I've known since I was born look at him with hearts in their eyes—especially when he flashes that wide smile of his. They practically fall over swooning at the smile, and the tattoos snaking down his arms give him just enough of an edge that he seems like the bad boy of their dreams.

He uses that smile to his advantage, whether it's to make old women swoon or to make younger women drop their panties. It works every time, the bastard.

Austin is still talking to Tiffany, which makes the skin on the back of my neck prickle. Tessa is off chatting with the crafters, who I'm sure are telling her what a great event this has been and how they want her to run it every year. Savannah is still slithering around here somewhere, and my eyes finally zero in on her laughing with Stephanie near Mrs. Burton's table.

Savannah and Stephanie. Now there's a duo that scares the shit out of me. All they need is to toss Tiffany into the mix, and then they'll really have a trio to be feared.

My heart picks up speed at the mere thought of the three of them talking earlier, but Tiffany is so enthralled by Austin that I doubt she'll leave his side to chat up Savannah and Stephanie, although I wouldn't put anything past Savannah. She digs until she knows everything, and that thought is nearly enough to propel me into action.

I force myself to lay low, though.

"Is that kid yours?" a voice to my left asks, and I glance over at Cory.

He's another guy I can trust, but he also knows I wasn't in the same zip code as Tessa when she would've gotten pregnant.

I nod. "In all the ways that matter."

He narrows his eyes at me. "Is that why you were riding our asses when you were in town a few weeks ago about settling down?"

I nod again.

"This is what you want? To be a father at twenty-five when you're young and good looking and a fucking NFL player who could have whatever pussy he wants?" he presses, asking the question I'm sure Travis was thinking but didn't have the audacity to ask.

I chuckle. "She's it for me, man. The only woman I've ever wanted."

He sighs. "What a huge disappointment you turned out to be."

I laugh. I know he's just teasing me. "Fuck off."

He slaps me on the shoulder. "I'm happy for you, man."

"Does this mean we're not going to be roommates when you get back to Vegas?" Travis asks, sauntering up behind me.

I shrug. "I hadn't really thought about that," I admit. "I bought her a house here in town. I don't know if she'll want to come to Vegas or stay here. We've been so wrapped up in planning this event that we haven't really had much chance to look beyond it."

"The offer's still on the table," he says. "Even if your dumb ass is committed to one woman, we'd still have a hell of a lot of fun."

It's a conversation Tessa and I need to have. If she wants to come with me, of course I'd rather live with her and the baby. But if she wants to stay here, I don't see much point in setting down roots in Vegas. It'll just be the place I go to work for a little over half the year.

I can't see her staying here without me, though I'd understand it. She'd be alone a great majority of the time with the baby if she came with me to a place where she knows literally nobody except me—and those friends of mine who made the trip out here for the festival. But at least here she'd have help from her mom.

"Thanks, man. I'm going to go see if she needs me to do anything," I say as we spot Tessa walking near the first auction table. The day has gone amazingly well, and the sun is starting to set. I have a feeling the party will go right up until ten o'clock, when the city has told us we have to pull the plug.

The deejay turns up the speakers a bit and a crowd gathers in front of his booth. The teenagers are dancing and having a good time. They're probably all drunk since that's what we would've done when we were their age. We would've gone out to the cornfields on the east side of town with a fifth of rum and drank ourselves silly. We might've gotten in trouble with our parents, or we might've slid under the radar.

I leave Cory and Travis so they can chat up the attendees, and I head over toward my girl, setting my hand on her lower back. "Everything okay?" I ask.

She nods, and she sets a hand on her hip as she leans back to stretch her stomach and back before running a hand along her stomach. "Yeah. I could sit for a few minutes. My body's aching, but otherwise, everything seems to be going well."

"I have a surprise," I say quietly.

She glances over at me, her brows furrowed. "What is it?"

"If I told you, it wouldn't be a surprise."

Her face lights up with a smile, and her eyes twinkle. "Tristan Higgins, what have you done?"

I laugh. "You'll see." I walk her over toward the Fallon Tavern since it's closest to where we are, and we find two empty chairs in the beer garden. I excuse myself to grab us a couple bottles of water, and when I sit back down, I hand one to her.

"Take it all in," I say, nodding toward the perfect view we have of Main Street.

We each drink our water quietly for a couple minutes as we watch the crowd.

Music, people dancing, others laughing, others walking and looking at the vendors. More laughter behind us in the beer garden. The streets are full, and business is booming. It's starting to get dark—the moment I've been waiting for seemingly for weeks.

It seems as though everyone from our little town made it out today, plus we have plenty of visitors from towns nearby. It's been a successful day, and it's all thanks to the gorgeous woman sitting beside me as we take it all in together.

"Pretty incredible, isn't it?" she asks.

I toss my arm around the back of her chair and lean in. I press a soft kiss to her neck. "Thank you for putting this together."

"Thank you for having the idea and trusting me to take it on. I had a blast doing the planning. I think it was exactly what I needed, but now I have to think about what's coming next."

I nod. "We will."

"There are just so many unanswered questions," she murmurs.

I grab her hand in mine. "There are, and we have time to answer all of them. Together."

She glances up at me, and our eyes connect meaningfully.

At that exact moment, the lights twined around the tree branches down Main Street go dark, and I know this is my moment.

Tessa gasps. "The lights!" she says, standing as she looks around frantically. "Are we losing power?"

And then the first burst of red illuminates the sky, followed by white and blue and purple. She stares up at the fireworks as they crackle and boom above us, and then she falls back into her seat.

She tears her eyes from the sky to look at me. "Fireworks? Did you do this?"

I offer a smile. "Surprise."

She punches me in the arm with a wide grin. "This is amazing."

We sit together and watch the first few, and then I take my moment while everyone's attention is overhead.

I get down on my knee and recite the cheesy line that I've been planning for weeks. "Tessa Taylor, you are all the fireworks I need. You light up my life in a way no one else has ever done, and I don't want to live another day without the promise that we'll spend forever together."

I pull the little box out of my pocket and flip it open, and she gasps as she looks at the ring.

"A princess cut surrounded by pave diamonds," we both say at the same time. It's the ring we saw on some television commercial when we were back in high school, and she told me she wanted it someday when she got engaged. I never forgot it.

"Will you marry me?" I ask as the fireworks continue to hiss, pop, and boom overhead.

She nods as tears sparkle in her eyes. "Yes. Oh my God, yes. Is this a dream?"

I slip the ring onto her finger, and she's crying and I have tears forming in my own eyes as emotion plows into me. She leans forward and puts her palms on my cheeks as she searches my eyes, and I feel this intense closeness with her in the moment, like she's searching into my soul, connecting and latching onto it since she's its other half.

I'm going to marry the only girl I've ever loved. We're having a baby together. We own the house on the corner.

She presses her lips to mine, and we seal our promise to each other while fireworks continue to pop overhead.

Could life get any better than this moment right now?

It's pure bliss that I know won't last forever, especially as I open my eyes and focus on my girl. I hardly feel the eyes on us. Tiffany Gable. Savannah Buck. Stephanie Taylor.

I thought maybe we could live in the bliss a little while longer.

I guess I was wrong.

CHAPTER 23

Tristan

The fireworks come to an end, and holy shit, I'm engaged to be married.

Again.

This engagement is real, though. It's meaningful and it's with the person I'm meant to be with. It's not a drunken mistake or a fear of being alone or a twisted way of getting what I think I need from the wrong person.

It's my Tessa.

We both stand at the conclusion of the fireworks, and she leans into my chest as the lights wrapped around the trees down the boulevard turn back on.

It's over. People are starting to file toward the exits, the crafters are cleaning up their tables, and the vendors are breaking down their displays.

I slide my arms around her. "Great work today. This event has been incredible."

She looks up at me, her eyes twinkling in the lights. "Because we did it together, Tristan," she says softly. "Remember when we were partners on projects in school? With your technical sense and my creative side, we aced every single one of them. Separate, we're just fragments of who we're meant to be, but together, we're T and T."

"We're dynamite," I whisper, leaning down to brush my lips across hers.

"Get a room!" a familiar voice calls beside us, and I laugh as I break apart, smiling at my buddies.

"Where are you staying?" I ask Travis, who just yelled at us.

"Some hotel in the Quad Cities. Ellie booked for all of us," he says. Cory, Patrick, Luke, and Ellie are huddled together on the sidewalk across the street.

"Where's Austin?"

"Still talking to that hot piece of ass—"

I cut him off with a glare and a slight incline of my head toward Tessa.

"I mean, still talking with that lovely lady from your town," he finishes.

"Lovely lady?" Tessa asks.

I sigh. "Tiff."

She wrinkles her nose. "Oh no."

"What?" Travis asks.

Tessa shakes her head. "Not a great choice."

"Why not?" he asks.

"She's…a lot. She's always been after Tristan, and she's basically the town gossip, so anything she does with Austin will be all over the internet by morning."

"I tried to warn him, but he ignored me." I shrug. "Live and learn, right?"

"And fix your mistakes," Tessa finishes, and I laugh as the others cross the street to join us.

"Is there anywhere to go around here?" Cory asks. "Maybe pick up some P?"

"Some P?" Tessa asks.

"Don't ask," I say, rolling my eyes. Then I lean in and whisper, "Pussy."

Her eyes widen a little. "You're in Fallon Ridge. You're not going to find much in these parts."

I shrug. "The dirty girls hang at the tavern. The wholesome ones hang at the Pizza Joint."

Tessa smacks me in the chest, but it's the truth.

"Which way to the tavern?" Cory asks, and everyone laughs as I point it out to him.

Everyone heads in that direction for a drink before heading out of town, and Tessa and I head in separate directions to help break everything down. The high school football players are busy folding chairs and breaking down tables, and the clean-up crew is already doing their thing.

I start collecting the signs we had custom made for this event. Maybe I can just store them in my parents' garage if we decide to do this again next year. I glance over at the cash booth and wonder how long it'll be before we learn the final totals when I feel an evil presence behind me.

I expect to find some feral cat, but when I turn around, it's just my ex-wife. "What do you want?" I ask, and my voice sounds tired even to my own ears.

"I know it's not your baby she's carrying," she says, putting her hands on her hips. "I know who it really belongs to."

"I'm tired of your games, Savannah. What do you want?"

She folds her arms across her chest. "Hm, let's see. What do I want to keep this information quiet?" She taps her chin as if she's deep in thought. "You, Tristan. I want *you*."

"So I give myself to you, and you keep quiet?" I ask.

She nods.

"Really, Savannah? Resorting to blackmail *again*?"

"It's not blackmail. It's just a persuasion tactic. I just want to be with you," she says, and her eyes are soft as she begs for an ounce of my attention. I *almost* feel bad for her, but then I remember how she's made my life a living hell for two years.

"Why? You know I don't love you."

"This isn't about *love*." She says the word with disdain, and I know she's got daddy issues or whatever, but I'm not sure I realized how far she'd fallen off the edge. This isn't any way to live life—not when I've experienced how it *should* be with Tessa. "How I feel about you, how you feel about me…it doesn't really matter. I hate that I've had two failed marriages, and I hate most of all that you were one of them. We were good together once upon a time, baby, and I just want to get there with you again."

"I can't keep doing this with you." I blow out a frustrated breath. "I asked Tessa to marry me. She's carrying my baby, and we own a house together, and that's it. She's my happily ever after. Cut the blackmail bullshit and get out of my life."

I turn to walk away, but her words stop me cold. "You sure you don't want to know the other things I've learned about your little girlfriend? Or what I know about you and a girl named Tiffany?"

I spin around to face her. "Fuck you, Savannah. I don't know why you get off on making me miserable, but it stops. Now. You utter one word of anybody's history to *anyone* and I'll have my lawyer throw you in jail so fast your fucking head will spin."

She laughs an evil cackle that draws goosebumps down my arms. "Nobody's going to throw me in jail for anything, sweet Tristan. There's nothing illegal about sharing my discoveries with anybody." She wiggles her fingers as she walks away. "Ta-ta for now."

I have no idea what I just unleashed, but I'm definitely worried about the potential consequences.

I'm standing in place, staring after her and debating whether I should chase after her and find some way to get her to stop this nonsense when my phone vibrates in my pocket.

Honest **MISTAKE**

I sigh. It doesn't matter, anyway. I have a better chance of stopping a moving freight train than stopping Savannah Dalton-Higgins-Buck when she's on a mission.

I glance at the text that just came through.

Ben Olson: *Heard your divorce is finalized. Making good on my promise to throw you a bash. I've got a two-day rager planned the weekend before minicamp—the only weekend Caesar's pool had two days open before camp. Friday and Saturday, see you then.*

He doesn't ask if that date works, but it doesn't matter if it works. If Ben Olson is planning you a party, you fucking clear your schedule so you can attend.

I search across Main Street for Tessa. As long as she can come with me, I don't see how that'll be a problem. It might be a nice surprise vacation to get away for a couple days after all the planning that went into this event.

I text him back.

Me: *I'll be there. Thanks, man.*

Now to convince Tessa to come with me.

CHAPTER 24

Tessa

I busy myself with chatting up the vendors, trying to push away the nagging nervousness that Savannah was talking to Tristan.

That Savannah was talking to Stephanie.

That Savannah was talking to Tiffany Gable.

That Savannah is here in my town at all, talking to my people and walking my streets and trying to steal Tristan away from me.

I don't know what this woman's obsession with my future husband is, but it's quite frankly terrifying.

I don't know what she's capable of, but I do know that she made Tristan miserable for a long time, and for that alone I want to punch the bitch.

It's been a wonderful but stressful day, and having these little issues skating around in the backdrop has only made it all the more stressful. My feet are killing me despite the gym shoes, and my back hurts despite the belly band. I'm ready to lie down for about a month, but I've also been having problems getting into a comfortable position since my hips hurt no matter which way I lay, and baby girl chooses my sleeping time for her soccer games.

I'm ready to walk home, but I'm waiting for Tristan, who's just finishing helping the high school kids pack up the tables and chairs. "I'll be by in the morning to unload," I hear him yell to Coach, and then he starts walking toward me.

I watch as he practically glides down the street. He makes even walking look graceful, something necessary for his agility when it comes to his sport. His scruff has grown in, and he's practically sporting a beard. His eyes find mine, and he runs a hand through his hair as he moves in my direction.

God, he's hot.

He links his hand through mine the second he gets to me. "Hey, future wife." He leans over and presses a soft kiss to my cheek, and I can't help my wide smile.

"Hey, future hubby."

He grins, too, and then we walk toward home. We both wave when we pass *our* house. I can't wait to move in. I can't wait to get started on our future together.

We turn down Oak Tree Lane.

"My buddy Ben is throwing me a divorce bash. He chose the weekend before the Aces minicamp in April. Want to come to Vegas with me to celebrate?" he asks.

I laugh. "Ben Olson?"

He nods.

"Oh, wow. I don't know if I can keep up with him. I've heard he throws some epic parties, and even if I *could* drink while I was there, I don't know if I'd fit in."

"Of course you would," he says softly. "You'll be there with me."

I squeeze his hand, and then we're walking up toward my front door.

"It sounds really fun. You're sure I wouldn't just be a third wheel or whatever?" I ask.

He nods. "I'm sure." He bends down to kiss me. "I want you there."

I nod. "Okay. Let's do it."

He grins. "I'm going to take a quick shower, but I'll check to see if you're still awake before bed. I'll need one more goodnight kiss. Or, you know, whatever you're up for."

I giggle. "I'm exhausted, but I'll leave my window unlocked so you can come in for that kiss."

He raises a brow and kisses me once more, and then he heads down the driveaway. I go inside, and the house is quiet and dark as I creep through it toward my room. I'm sure my mom is already asleep—I saw her walking back home with Sue and Russ just after the fireworks, so she's probably been home an hour by now, which means she's in that sort of deep sleep that she's impossible to wake from…the perfect time for Tristan to come back and see *exactly* what I'm up for.

But first, a shower is a great idea.

I grab my towel and head into the bathroom, and it's when I peel off my clothes that something feels all wrong.

I glance down at my underwear and spot a pool of bright red blood.

I feel a little dizzy for a second, so I grab onto the counter and draw in a deep breath.

It's a lot of blood, and fear paralyzes me for a second. I don't get queasy at the sight or anything like that—in my line of work, I can't—but when it's coming from my body while I'm pregnant, icy terror grips my heart.

I sit on the toilet as I try to figure out what to do, and then a single thought flashes through my brain.

Call Tristan.

I reach for my jeans and fish my phone out, and I dial his number. He doesn't pick up right away, and just before I'm sure it'll go to voicemail, he catches it.

He's out of breath. "Sorry! I was just getting in the shower when I saw you were calling. What's up?"

My voice comes out small and scared. "I—I'm bleeding."

"Bleeding?" he asks. He sounds confused.

"The baby—I'm scared, Tristan. It's a lot of blood."

"I'll be right there."

I stay where I am on the toilet, and less than a minute later, the bathroom door opens. In the back of my mind, I feel like I should be embarrassed that Tristan is walking in while I'm sitting naked on a toilet, but I can't find it in me to care when I'm so scared about the reason why I might be bleeding.

He runs to me and wraps his arms around me, but I don't miss when his eyes widen as they catch on my underwear still on the floor.

"Do you feel okay?" he asks, and I nod. "Does anything hurt?"

I shake my head. "I'm just scared," I say softly.

"Let's get you to the ER, okay?" he asks gently. "Where can I find you some clean underwear?"

"Top left drawer of my dresser."

He runs to my bedroom and returns a minute later. "Do you have any pads?"

I nod toward the bathroom cabinet, and he hands me one. He turns around to give me privacy while I get dressed again, and once he hears me washing my hands, he wraps an arm around me. He waits until I'm done, and then he carries me through the house and out to his truck. "Do you want me to wake your mom?" he asks before he starts the truck.

I shake my head. "Let her sleep. No reason to worry her until we hear from the doctor."

He speeds through toward the Quad Cities, since the emergency room there is slightly closer than Davenport, and his tires screech as he pulls into the parking lot at the emergency room. "Can you walk?" he asks as he runs around to open my door, and I nod.

We check in and it's fairly empty, so I'm taken back to a room right away. "Are you the father?" the tech asks Tristan, and he nods. It's complicated, but at the same time, it's the truth.

They take my vitals, ask me about a million questions, stick a needle in my hand to hook me up to an IV, and the doctor comes in a few minutes later.

"We're going to run a quick ultrasound," she says, and she looks at Tristan. "You'll need to stay here." He opens his mouth to object the same time I do, but she holds up a hand. "I know you want to go back there, but it's hospital policy. She'll go into a room, have the ultrasound, and then she'll come back here. We'll wait for radiology to read the results and send them to me, and then I will report back with our findings." She's firm but kind, and I appreciate the fact that she's so controlled when everything feels chaotic.

I'm wheeled back to the ultrasound room, and they run the test for me. There's no screen in here, no speakers for me to listen to the baby's heartbeat, so I have no idea whether everything is okay or not.

And then I'm wheeled back.

"If avoiding stress is one of the recommendations, they should really not do this to pregnant women," I mutter to Tristan while we wait.

He squeezes my hand and presses a kiss to my temple. "Whatever they tell us, I'm right here."

It's a full forty-five minutes before the doctor returns. "The baby is fine," she begins. "Nice, strong heartbeat. Growth is normal, and development is right on track. It looks like you've got a low-lying placenta. It *could* shift into previa, so my recommendation is definitely pelvic rest, and I'd even recommend bedrest for you."

"Bedrest?" I repeat at the same time Tristan asks, "What's previa?"

"When the placenta covers the opening of the cervix," she explains. "It could become dangerous for both baby and mother, and it does shift to previa for about one in ten pregnant women diagnosed with a low-lying placenta. Usually risk factors include previous deliveries. Is this your first baby?" the doctor asks.

My eyes widen and my face blanches as I try to figure out how to answer that question.

I have things I haven't told Tristan, yet he's here with me. I don't want to lie to the doctor…but I also can't admit the truth. Not right now.

"Mm-hm," I lie, and I try to convey to the doctor that I'm lying without letting Tristan in on it.

It doesn't work. She just gives me a weird look, but since it won't change the treatment, I'm not sure the cause matters. The only thing I have on my side here is the fact that I'm a nurse and while I know causes are important, treatment is more important.

I can fill in my regular doctor on the rest, especially since I can predict her next sentence.

"Make sure you see your OB in the next few days. They'll run another ultrasound and just check that everything's okay. We can send your paperwork right over."

I make a mental note to call the office ahead of time and explain the situation.

Or maybe I should just tell Tristan the truth.

My brand-new princess cut diamond sparkles in the light. Aside from this visit to the emergency room, everything is going so well between us. It's pure bliss. It's everything I dreamed of since I was twelve.

I want to tell him, but I'm too scared of the potential consequences…especially after everything we've been through tonight.

CHAPTER 25

Tristan

I keep my hand firmly planted in hers as the doctor tells us her diagnosis, as she answers questions and pays her fee, as she's released, as we walk out to the car, and the entire drive back home.

The blood scared me.

She was right…it was a lot.

But the way my instincts took over tell me I can do this. Every first-time parent is scared. It's natural. But when the baby is in danger, you set aside that fear and adrenaline kicks in.

I feel like once the baby is here, that's pretty much what it'll be like. A balance between fear and adrenaline.

She clears her throat, breaking the silence as we both recover from that fear mixed with adrenaline in the car on the way home.

"So I guess I can't go to Vegas with you," she murmurs.

I squeeze her hand where I still clutch it. "It's okay. I'll just text Ben and tell him I can't come."

She shakes her head. "No, no. Don't do that. This is your big bash, and you deserve to celebrate the fact that she's not your wife anymore."

"I'd rather celebrate that with you," I murmur, and she squirms a little.

"The doctor said pelvic rest," she says, regret in her tone. "So as much as I wish I could take you up on that, we're going to have to wait."

"I didn't mean sex," I amend. "I just like spending time with you." Although if I would've known that the quickie in our new kitchen today would've been the last time for a while, I might've taken my time instead of ravaging her the way I did.

"I like spending time with you, too. It feels like we're already back to where we were, like we paused for a bit but picked up where we were supposed to." She glances over at me.

"I feel that too," I say. "We're like a boring old married couple already."

She laughs. "I'd hardly call us boring. Me knocked up, you a celebrity…it's always going to be a little chaotic for us, isn't it?"

I shake my head. "Not when we're at our home in Fallon Ridge. It's our happy place. The calm amidst the chaos."

"Fallon," she says suddenly out of the blue.

"Fallon?" I repeat.

"Fallon Higgins," she says as if she's trying it on for size.

"Fallon Higgins," I repeat. "Wait…Higgins?"

"If it's going to be my last name, it's going to be her last name. I looked into adding you as the father on the birth certificate. I can't legally list someone other than her biological father, but there's a special affidavit we can complete to make it legal." She squeezes my hand. "You'll be her father in all the ways that matter."

I wish I wasn't driving so I could take her in my arms at her words, so we could seal that promise with a kiss. It's everything I ever wanted with the one person I ever wanted it with.

"Thank you," I say softly instead.

Honest MISTAKE

We pull onto Oak Tree Lane, and I help her inside. I take her all the way to her bathroom, and I help her into the shower. I clean up the bathroom, tossing her bloody underwear into the garbage can, and then I join her in the shower. I press my lips softly to hers before I fill the loofah with her jasmine soap and wash away the day—both the good parts, like the festival, and the hard parts, like the ER visit.

The bubbles swirl down the drain, and I pull her closer to me. "I love you," I say, and then I take her mouth with mine. My dick is hard for her like always, and it presses into the side of her belly between us.

She pulls back breathlessly after a moment, her chest rising and falling as she pants. "I love you, too. But I'm on pelvic rest, and kissing like that when we're already naked is only going to lead to things that are not very restful for my pelvis."

I chuckle, and I press a soft kiss to her lips again. "I'll finish up in here, then," I say, and she gets out to dry off while I scrub myself clean, the scent of her jasmine on my skin a total turn-on. Once she steps out of the bathroom to get some clothes out of her room, I take care of business. The soap is nice and slippery, and combined with the water while I stroke myself, it isn't long before I'm coming all over my hand.

I wash the mess away down the drain, and then I get out of the shower, much more relaxed than when I stepped into the bathroom four hours ago after a frantic phone call.

She's already asleep by the time I get out of the shower. I throw on my dirty clothes, run home to change into clean shorts and a t-shirt, and slip back into her window.

And then I hold her in my arms until morning.

I wake to the sound of my phone buzzing on the nightstand beside me. It's only eight—too early given the fact that we didn't go to bed until well after four in the morning—so I grab my phone to silence it before it wakes Tessa up.

I check it, and I have a bunch of missed calls and text messages from Ellie.

I look through the texts.

The first couple were from last night.

Ellie: *The festival was incredible. I posted a bunch of photos on your social media.*

Ellie: *Did you find out the total amount raised yet? I'd like to post that, too.*

And the next few came through this morning.

Ellie: *Did you see all the attention on your Instagram?*

Ellie: *Can we meet somewhere for breakfast so I can go over a few things with you?*

Ellie: *Our flight leaves at three, so we'll be getting on the road toward Chicago around noon.*

Ellie: *You just crossed one million followers on Instagram.*

One million?

I was just at eight hundred thousand last I checked a month or so ago.

What happened? What, exactly, has Ellie been posting?

I open the social media app to take a look for myself, and I see a bunch of photos from the Aces weight room. All ones where I'm not wearing a shirt or where my biceps are highlighted.

I mean…I'm proud of my biceps. I'm proud of my abdomen. I work my ass off in the gym and I try to eat right most of the time so I'm in peak physical condition for my performances on the field.

But I'd never post these photos of myself. I guess that's why I hired Ellie. She knows what attracts people, and the more followers I have on my social media platforms, the more offers start to roll in.

And the more…*inappropriate* the comments become.

Honest **MISTAKE**

Some are just emojis. Water droplets or hearts. Some offer marriage, and others offer a bed. But none of them are appropriate things you'd say to someone engaged to another woman.

It's part of the territory, I guess. It's just the part I've never gotten accustomed to. I'm still trying to figure all this out, and I spent the first two years of it married to the wrong woman. I'll spend the rest of my career married to the right one.

Ellie's made mention of how appealing to the female audience is what will grow my account, but is it worth the price? Is it worth appealing to the females and allowing them to think they've got a shot with me when they just don't?

I scroll through my photos from yesterday and decide to post one of my own. It's not curated by my publicist, but this is *my* account and I want people to know how goddamn happy I am…and how there's not a chance in hell for anybody else.

She hasn't even had a chance to tell her mom that we're engaged yet. Between the festival and the emergency room, it's been a whirlwind. So I don't post a ring as my caption, but I do find a selfie of the two of us cheesing for the camera. I think about what to write, and I finally settle on keeping it simple.

Finally back with the love of my life.

I post the picture and close the app, and then I text Ellie.

Me: *I can meet you in the Quad Cities in about a half hour. There's a diner just around the corner from your hotel.*

She texts back right away confirming our breakfast date, and I slip quietly out of bed. Despite my efforts not to wake her, she rustles. "Where are you going?" she whispers sleepily.

"Ellie asked if I could meet her for breakfast before they head back to Vegas," I say. "You're more than welcome to come with, but you need your rest."

"I can rest all day. Let's go get some food," she says, sitting up and wincing a little.

I rush over. "Is everything okay?"

She nods. "My hips just kill me in this bed. The mattress is just so unforgivingly firm."

I make a mental note to get a better mattress for our house.

"Maybe you should sleep at my house the next few days until we can move into our house. My mattress is much softer."

"That's a good idea. I was thinking the recliner in the family room might work, too. When are you meeting Ellie?" she asks.

"I'll run home to change and meet you out front in ten minutes. Does that work?" I ask.

She nods, and I climb out the window.

Ten minutes later, I'm standing by the truck as she walks out the front door. Her mom is already at church since it's a Sunday morning, and the roads are quiet through town as we make our way to the highway.

"Hard to believe there was a huge festival here yesterday. The clean-up crew did an amazing job," she muses.

"I think the person who assigned the clean-up crew is the one who did an amazing job," I counter, and she blushes a little. "Would you do this again?"

"The festival?" she clarifies.

I nod.

"Yeah, I would." She glances around at the shops and restaurants down Main Street. "It was a lot of work, but it was so much fun planning it. I already have ideas for next year, and I'd love to talk to some of the attendees and get a handle on what they thought went well, what they thought we could change. That sort of thing. I'd like to get the local businesses even more involved, but they really showed up for us yesterday."

"Did you ever get a final total?" I ask.

She nods. "Darlene sent me a screenshot of her spreadsheet." She opens her phone and starts reading from the email Darlene, the accountant who volunteered her efforts for our event, sent. "We sold a little over twenty-seven hundred tickets at five bucks apiece. The auction raised seven thousand, the raffle was six, and the games raised about twelve hundred. With other donations, we're looking at giving Landon's family just under thirty thousand dollars."

"Holy shit," I whisper. A feeling of pride permeates my chest. *We did that.*

I can't even imagine how much that will help Landon and his family, and I want to do it again. Year after year, I want to find a way to give back to the community I love so much. *Our* community.

"Incredible, right?"

I glance over at her and catch her eye. "Yeah," I murmur. "You sure are."

CHAPTER 26

Tessa

I close the email from Darlene and spot yet another notification from Instagram.

I rarely post there. I'm more of a silent scroller myself, less likely to draw attention to what I'm doing than to post the highlight reel.

I have a bunch of messages, and I spot Sara's name first. I click on it to read what she sent me.

Sara: *You're the love of his life? How come I never knew about this???*

I click the link she attached, and it takes me to a photo posted by Tristan Higgins this morning.

We look so damn happy in the picture, and that's my first thought.

It's the second thought that comes out my mouth. "You posted a picture of us?" My tone is one of surprise.

His eyes edge over to me. "Is that not okay?"

"It's…fine, I guess." I guess I'm not sure how to feel about it. On the one hand, I want to shout from the rooftops that he's mine and everyone else should stay the hell away. On the other hand, I don't need anyone else sniffing around me or my history—especially since I told him I wasn't interested in the spotlight. "It's just, my inbox is blowing up and it took me off guard a little."

"I'm sorry," he murmurs. He reaches over and squeezes my leg. "I had all these comments from women, and I guess I just wanted to shut them down. To let them know I'm with somebody. I never really thought twice about it. I didn't post the engagement ring because I figured you'd want to tell your mom first."

"Thanks." My tone is flat as I realize I've been engaged for nearly twelve hours and my mom still doesn't know. I've also been to the emergency room and back and even slept a couple hours…also things my mother isn't aware of.

I sigh.

"You're mad," he says softly.

"I'm not." I shake my head as I reach over and lay a hand on his thigh. How could I be mad after he held my hand through the whole emergency room visit last night? How could I be mad after he bought me a house? It's just a picture on Instagram and it blindsided me a little. "It's all just a little overwhelming."

"Do you want to skip breakfast?" he asks.

"No, no. Not at all. I love seeing you with your friends. It's a new Tristan—you're in your element. You're smiling. It's not so heavy all the time, you know?"

He nods. "That's what friends are for, I think."

"I'd love to see them again before they leave." I pause as I think about how I'd like to see them in Vegas, too. "I'm sorry I won't be able to go to Vegas with you."

"I think I should cancel," he says. "Stay back and make sure you're okay. I won't enjoy it anyway. I'll be thinking about you the whole time if you're not there."

"I'm fine, Tristan. The baby's fine, too. Your trip is still a couple weeks away anyway, and we'll get that second opinion this week with my doctor. Aren't you going back for minicamp the next weekend anyway?" I ask.

"Yeah. I think you should come to Vegas. We can drive, or we can find a way to travel safely. That way I can keep an eye on you."

My chest aches as I think how much I want that. Part of me wants him to stay here forever, but I'd never really ask him for that. He's got a job to do, and the minicamps and OTAs are all part of it. He'll go for his workouts, but he'll be back after a long weekend away. Then he'll go for OTAs, but again, he'll come back. It's when training camp starts in late July…that's the time I'm worried about.

That's the time I think I should go with him.

That's the time I'll have a newborn with me to consider, too, and I want her to be with him. I want her to bond with him. I want them to get to know each other even if he's gone all day and only home a few hours each night.

I want him for those hours, too.

I don't mention all that. I keep telling myself we have lots of time.

But time is this strange phenomenon that just doesn't slow down no matter how much we want it to.

Eventually he'll go back, and I have to figure out what comes next for the baby and me. If I leave Fallon Ridge to go to Vegas, I leave my mom behind. But I've already started over in this life more than once. I'm strong enough to do it again with Tristan as part of the equation—even if it means quiet days and lonely nights.

I just wish I had some direction beyond becoming a mother. I wish I wanted to go back to nursing, but I don't. I don't miss it, not the way I thought I would.

The more I think about it, the more I realize how much I enjoyed planning the festival. I'd love to do more things like that for charity—for the TNT Higs Foundation. For *our* charity.

It still feels surreal that it even exists as a possibility.

"You're quiet," he murmurs as we pull into the parking lot.

"I'm sorry." I glance over at him but I avert my gaze to the windshield when I blurt, "I'm just thinking about what happens next."

"Next?" he asks.

"When you have to go back to Vegas," I clarify. "Not these short weekends away, but for training camp and the entire season."

He nods, and then he reaches over to grab my hand. "Come with me."

My brow furrows as I meet his eyes. "I'll have a newborn. I'll be all alone."

He shakes his head as he reaches over to grab my hand. "You won't be alone. I will be right there, and when I can't be there, you'll have Ellie. Jack, my quarterback, has little kids, and Ben Olson's wife just had twins. It's a family, Tessa, and I want you to be part of it. We're engaged to be married, and I want you walking by my side for all of it."

"But Ellie and Jack and Ben…they're all *actual* family, right?" I know the history. Ellie's married to Jack's brother. Ben's married to Jack's sister. "I'll just be an outsider looking in."

"You won't be," he says, his tone adamant. "Sure, they have actual family relations, but they're not the only ones on the team with kids. Coach is like our team father, and his wife, Mo, is like the team mother. They've built a program where we all rely on each other both on and off the field. Trust me, Tess. You won't be alone. Ever."

What he's saying…it all sounds so good. It sounds wonderful, actually. I've spent so much of the last few years feeling alone, like I hardly had any family at all since I stayed away except for the occasional calls with my mom.

But we're close now, and the thought of leaving her again is scary.

"I'll think about it," I say. "But Tristan?"

His eyes meet mine and he raises his brows.

"I don't want to be in the spotlight." My voice is quiet, and I heave in a deep breath as the confession leaves me feeling a little uneasy about our future together. "Is that okay? I don't want people finding out who the father is. I don't want people looking into my private affairs. I don't want a loud life where every detail is picked apart in the media."

He nods. "I don't want any of that either, and that's part of why I bought the Cunningham's house for us. Fallon Ridge just feels like the right place for us. It's quiet and far from the spotlight. I will do whatever I can to protect you from it. I'm not immune, but plenty of guys and their families live this life without the constant media frenzy."

I nod, and he leans across the console to press his lips to mine.

We head inside, where four football players and Ellie sit in a corner booth waiting for us. The men all wear ballcaps pulled down low as if it'll disguise their identity, but I'd venture a guess that it's not often four—now five—professional athletes who are essentially tall, hulking men walk into the corner diner in Moline, Illinois.

The server seems nervous as she approaches our table to get our drink order. She's young—late teens or early twenties, I'd guess, and it's like she knows these men are all somebody, but she hasn't figured out who exactly they are just yet.

I order some orange juice after Tristan orders water and coffee, and then I glance over at the guys. They're all deep in conversation already, so I lean toward her with a conspiratorial smile. "They're all players for the Vegas Aces," I whisper, and her cheeks turn bright red.

"I'll be r-r-right back with your d-d-drinks," she stammers, and it's this very moment I realize how freaking lucky I am to be sitting at this table.

I'm part of the inner circle.

I *belong* here.

Tristan took me under his wing when I was new to Fallon Ridge, and I don't know why I doubted for even a second that he wouldn't do the exact same thing in Vegas.

And with that thought in mind, the decision is made.

I'll stay here to have the baby…but come July, I'm moving to Vegas.

CHAPTER 27

Tristan

My chest relaxes a little as I watch Tessa chat comfortably with Ellie. Ellie can make conversation with just about anybody, but I feel like Tessa needed this. She needed to see that we're just a group of normal people who happen to play a televised sport each week in season.

I catch snippets here and there of their conversation—mostly stuff about being pregnant. She tells Ellie about our scare last night, about the pelvic rest…about all of it. I'm trying to stay engaged with the story Cory is relaying to us about some chick he hooked up with last week, but my ear catches on something Ellie says to Tessa.

"You're more than welcome to move in with us a while if you decide to come to Vegas. It's becoming a house of chaos, but I wouldn't have it any other way."

A look of relief seems to pass over Tessa's face at the offer. I know she's worried she'll move to Vegas with me only to find herself completely alone, but I'd never allow that.

I want to get us a house, but I need to hold out for confirmation that I'll be in Vegas another year. I even thought for a brief moment that if I could just get her out there with me, she'd want to move there.

Palm trees, mountains, bright lights, warm weather in the winter, views for days…there's a lot to love about the little desert oasis. When I first moved out, I felt like I was always on vacation. Savannah managed to ruin that for me, but when I get a minute to take a deep breath of desert air (provided it's not June, July, or August), it still feels that way for me, too.

I don't have a place, and I'm certain Travis won't want me to move in if I'm bringing not just a girl but a *baby* with me…so maybe this is the perfect solution.

"What do you say, Higs?"

"Higs?"

"Tristan!"

Somewhere in my periphery, the male voices at my table turn back to full volume and I realize Cory's trying to get my attention.

"Huh?" I ask, turning back toward my friends. Cory rolls his eyes while Austin and Travis laugh.

"I asked where you're staying the weekend of the Big D Bash," Cory says.

"Is that what Olson is calling it?" I ask, and Cory nods. I laugh. "I haven't thought about it. I turned my keys in to my landlord, so my house isn't an option. I'll probably just get a suite at Caesar's."

"Get it quick because it's booking up fast," Cory warns. "The only reason Ben got the pool reserved when he did is because there was supposed to be some wedding that weekend and the bride decided the groom's brother was a better fit."

"Jesus," I mutter.

"Kind of funny that it went from a wedding party to a divorce party just that fast," Patrick says.

Funny in an ironic way, I guess.

I'm starting to think I don't really want this party at all. My life feels so different than it did not so long ago when I asked

Ben to throw me a party once my divorce was finalized. I don't want to be the center of attention. I don't want bikini-clad women hanging on my every move for two days straight.

It sounded good when I was married to the devil and the woman I loved was just a distant memory.

But now she's back in my life, and I just want to soak up every second I can with her. I just want to get ready for our baby's arrival. I just want to take care of her and make sure she's okay, the baby's okay, we're okay.

Instead, I'm heading to Vegas under false pretenses. I'll get wasted, sure—but all the hook-ups I was expecting at my Big D Bash will be reserved for my friends. I'll be heading back to my suite alone, wishing my girl was with me.

It sounds so dramatic, but my life changed the second I spotted Tessa Taylor in the window across the yard a little over two months ago.

A divorce is a huge, life-altering event.

Falling in love is a huge, life-altering event

An engagement is a huge, life-altering event.

A baby is a huge, life-altering event.

And these events are things I'm going through all at the same time.

In the car on the way home, I broach the topic before she does. "I heard Ellie mention we could stay with them a while. What do you think about that?"

She clears her throat, and then she glances over at me. "I'm not sure why I worried for even a second that I'd be alone. You found a way to make me feel like a part of Fallon Ridge when I first moved here, and I know you'd do it again in Vegas. It's just…different this time. I'll have a baby, and I'll be a new mom, and it's all so scary to think about."

I nod. "I get it. Having your mom close would be helpful for sure. And my parents, too."

"Yeah," she murmurs, and then she pauses before she glances over at me. And then her words come tumbling out in a blur. "Or having Ellie around to bounce ideas and questions off of since she has two little kids, not to mention her nanny who takes care of the kids and their cousins while the moms work, might be pretty incredible, too, you know, while I'm planning more events for the TNT Higs Foundation."

My brows knit together as I try to process everything she just said, and I find I can't.

We're on the highway doing eighty, and I pull off at the next exit. I pull off on the shoulder and put the car in park.

"Can you break that down for me one more time?" I ask.

She laughs a little nervously. "Well, for starters, I want to move to Vegas with you."

My chest feels like it's been tight for weeks, but her words make the weight lift. I relax back into my seat.

"I think it might be nice to stay with Ellie and Luke a while. I don't know her that well, but I feel like she could become a good friend. I feel like it's someone I immediately trust, someone who could help guide me through this motherhood thing so I don't feel so alone."

I nod. "Luke doesn't play anymore, but they're both still involved in the sport. Kate is over there all the time, and so is Kaylee, and all of them have newborns. All girls, now that I think about it."

"Kate and Kaylee?" she asks.

"Kate Dalton is Jack Dalton's wife and Ellie's sister-in-law and best friend forever. And Kaylee is Ben Olson's wife and she's Luke and Jack's little sister," I explain.

She nods as she figures out the puzzle in her head. "Ellie was telling me she works from home and she has a nanny that watches her kids and her nieces and nephews during the day, so that must be who she was talking about."

"Are you sure you want to live with them and not just get our own place?" I ask.

"I do want to get our own place eventually, but for the initial move, I think it might be nice to stay with somebody we know. What if it doesn't work out?"

"What if *what* doesn't work out?" I ask. The thought that *we* might not work out never even crossed my mind.

"Moving to Vegas. What if I hate being away from my mom, or if I have post-partum depression, or if I just feel all alone with a newborn? There's so much change, so many variables, and I just want to make sure Vegas is a good fit before we invest in something as expensive as real estate."

I nod, and I wipe my forehead in jest. "You scared me there for a second."

"I did?" she asks.

I nod. "When you said what if it doesn't work out, I thought you meant *us*."

She's quiet a beat, and then her eyes move to mine. They're full of heat, but they're somehow soft at the same time. "I never doubted us for a second." Her voice is soft.

I lean over the console and press my lips to hers, and then my palm comes up to cup her neck, drawing her closer to me as I deepen the kiss. She tastes like cinnamon and syrup, and the sweet combination mixed with our fiery kiss only makes me want her more.

Pelvic rest, Higgins, I remind myself.

I begrudgingly back off, slowing the kiss before pressing one more soft one there since I can't get enough.

"I never did, either," I admit. "I knew there'd be obstacles, and it wouldn't be easy, but I knew somewhere down the road, we'd find our way back. It was inevitable."

She draws in a breath then releases it in a contented sigh, like she's letting go of whatever fears remain. "And the TNT Higs thing?" she asks.

I can't help when my lips tip up into a smile. "You know, I need a foundation director. You know anybody who might be up to the task?"

She raises her hand. "Me?"

I chuckle. "You're hired. We'll figure out the pay and all that later. I'll need to get my lawyer and CPA involved because I have no idea how foundations work, but I do know you can draw a salary."

She shakes her head. "I'm not worried about a salary. I can always run the foundation separately and work another job, too."

"Nursing?" I ask, and I rush to add, "If that's what you want, that's what I want for you. But you don't seem all that excited to return to nursing, and running the foundation would allow you to work at your own pace and work from home."

Her eyes light up. "Not nursing. Ellie mentioned that she could use some extra hands at her PR firm. She specifically said she'd love to work with someone who already has some experience planning an event for a foundation."

I raise my brows. "So she offered you a job *and* a place to live over breakfast?"

She laughs. "Yeah, I guess she did."

I lean in and kiss her again. It feels like it's already working out and we haven't even left the Midwest yet.

And that's the whole problem. I'm so blinded by the excitement of it all falling into place that I never even saw the blindside coming for us.

CHAPTER 28

Tessa

"We have some news," I say to my mom later in the afternoon. Tristan's arm is around me and we're snuggling on the couch when my mom walks in from her day at the church.

She looks between us, and her lips widen into a smile before her eyes dart down to my left hand. "I knew it!"

I can't help my smile, too, as I stand. "We're getting married."

She throws her arms around me. "I'm so happy for you. Congratulations."

She hugs Tristan next. "You're just so perfect for her, and I was always rooting for you two to end up together."

"Thanks, Mrs. Taylor," he says.

"Stop it, Tristan. It's Janet, or Jan, or Mom. Even Mil if you want."

"Mil?" Tristan repeats.

"Mother-in-law," she clarifies, and we all laugh.

"Mil it is," he says.

"Tell me everything. How'd he do it?"

I glance at Tristan as she slides onto the recliner angled beside the couch, and he nods almost imperceptibly. It's a silent form of communication that I've always had with him, like we can have an entire conversation without a single word.

"Oh, gosh, we have so much to tell you, Mom. He did it last night during the fireworks," I begin.

"Oh, man! I was walking back home with Sue and Russ. Wait, do they know?"

Tristan shakes his head.

"Not yet," I say. "Last night when we got in, I went to take a shower, and there was…I mean, *I* was…bleeding." She gasps. "Everything's totally fine," I assure her, "but Tristan rushed me to the emergency room to get me checked. I have what's called a low-lying placenta and there's like a ten percent chance it could turn into something else but the doctor recommended pelvic rest and general rest. We'll be okay."

She puts her hand on her chest like my words are an actual relief. "Oh my goodness, Tessi-cat. You should've woken me up. I could've been there too…" Her words trail off at the end as it seems like some realization plows into her. "But Tristan was there. Just as he should have been." Her eyes meet his, and she smiles a little sadly. "Thank you for being there for my girl—my girls."

"I wouldn't have been anywhere else," he says.

My mom glances between us, and I feel like she has something she wants to say.

I nod. "It's okay, Mom. We're ready to answer the tough questions, and I can tell you have one."

She hesitates, and then she lets it fly as her eyes lock on mine. "Will you be moving to Vegas with him for the season, then?"

I clear my throat and glance at him, and my eyes are locked on his when I answer, "Yes."

He squeezes my hand.

"Oh," she says softly.

"I have some good friends who've invited us to stay with them," Tristan says. "A husband and wife. She's my publicist, actually, and they have two small children and childcare. She works from home and has already offered Tessa a job."

My mom's brows shoot up. "Wow. You've already got it all figured out."

"We're working on it," I say. "And there will always be a place for you to come visit. We have our house here when we're in the off-season. We'll be sort of like snowbirds, right? Except we'll be coming back at the end of winter."

"Snowbirds," my mom echoes.

I glance at Tristan, and he nods again. "Come with us," I say softly.

"You know I can't," she says. "I've got my job at the church, and Bingo, and the Ladies' Auxiliary. I can't just leave."

Tristan reaches over and grabs my mom's hand. "It'll be okay," he says softly. "They'll be okay. My mom has been ducking in and out for the last few years so she can come to my games in Vegas. They commute back and forth, and there's always a ticket available for you if you'd ever like to join."

She brushes away a tear. "I just—I just—" She puts a hand over her mouth as she lets out a little sob.

I stand, walk over, and kneel beside her. "What is it, Mama?"

"What if there's a problem and he's out of town for the weekend?" she asks. "He says there's no other place he would have been last night, but what if something like that happened in-season?" She bites her lip to keep the tears at bay.

"Trust me, it's something I've thought about, too," I say. "Be ready for anything, right? But Ellie will be there. I'll be living with someone who's a mother to two young children, and Tristan's entire team will be there standing by us, ready to support us if we need anything at all."

"But that's not a replacement for your mother," my mom says quietly, and I press my lips together.

"You're right. That's why I want you to come with us, and if you can't or won't, that's okay. You come visit all the time," I say.

She shakes her head. "I can't just come visit and stay in somebody else's home."

"My parents love staying on the Strip when they come visit," Tristan says. "Their favorite place is the Flamingo. Something about how it always smells like coconuts there. You pick the place, and I'll book you the room."

"You don't have to do all that," she protests weakly.

Tristan chuckles as he stands. He walks over and kneels next to her, mirroring me, but then he tosses his arm around her shoulder. "You're about to be my MIL. You're family, Janet, and it's my way of thanking you for your daughter."

Well, that starts the waterworks again—only this time it's both my mother *and* me.

My mom invites Tristan's parents over for dinner so we can tell them, too, and they both have knowing smiles before we open our mouths to make our confession.

"I asked Tessa to marry me," Tristan announces as soon as they walk in the front door, and hugs and kisses are issued all around.

I even hear my mom say, "We're going to be family!" to Sue.

My mom orders in pizza and salads from the Pizza Joint and we all sit around the table chatting as we wait for it to arrive.

They ask all the same questions, and Russ says at one point to my mom, "We should look into buying a place we can share when we're out there visiting our kids and grandchild."

I'm not crying, I swear.

Okay, I'm crying just a little.

He just called the baby their *grandchild*. They look at this baby that Tristan has taken on as his own as theirs, too, and the thought melts my heart.

"I have about a million questions," Sue says, but then she looks over at me. "But let's start with this one. Are you sure you're okay with the life he leads? It's a lot different there in Vegas than here in Fallon Ridge."

I smile and nod as he grabs my hand in his. "I'm sure," I say softly.

I say the word on the outside…but on the inside, I'm nervous. I still don't know what, exactly, his life is like now, and I don't know what it'll be like when we just want to pop over to the market or go try on shoes at the mall or head to the movie theater. Will paparazzi follow us everywhere? Will they be camped outside to snap pics of the happy family walking out of their home? Or have I way over-glamorized this in my head?

Time will tell, I guess, but even though I say I'm sure about this new lifestyle…there's only one thing I'm certain about, and that's Tristan.

The rest I'm actually not so sure about.

CHAPTER 29

Tristan

The weeks seem to fly by even though she's been on modified bed rest. We present the check to Landon's family, which is a quiet affair since I know how prideful the family is. Still, it's life-changing, and Tessa cries as we hand it over while I swallow down the lump in my throat.

We did that.

We helped them, and we helped change their lives.

Something about the two of us coming together to plan this event that benefitted not just Landon's family but the entire town of Fallon Ridge causes some feeling beyond pride to bloom in my chest. When the two of us join forces—T and T—it's explosive, and I feel the future within our grasp as we work together to do more good.

But for now, we rest. We binge shows on Netflix. We eat popcorn and she watches me work out. We order furniture for our new home. She helps me stretch my hamstring, which is feeling better and better every day, and she rests, too, after that scary emergency room visit.

We decide on July seventh as our move-in date. The baby will be almost a month old by then, God willing, and it's three weeks until camp starts so it gives us some time to get adjusted to our new life together as she gets to know a completely new town.

Her obstetrician warned her to stay on pelvic rest for the next few weeks, and she has to attend weekly appointments to check the placenta placement. She said it was probably okay for her to travel to Vegas, but we decided not to risk it since she needs to check in with the doctor each week. The doctor also told her to take it easy, so it's not really bed rest, but it's not really normal activity, either.

I find myself boarding a plane after a difficult goodbye. I don't want to attend my Big D Bash. I don't want to fake like I'm a happy bachelor partying it up when my girl isn't even here with me.

And so that's why I was honest with Ben. I explained to him via text message that I'm already engaged to another woman, that we're having a baby together, that the situation is complicated but I'm not coming to Vegas for a huge weekend of hook-ups.

He was totally understanding, and while it's still the Big D Bash since it's all about celebrating my divorce, it's also about celebrating the off-season with all our buddies. So the Big D also stands for Drinks. Defense. Dudes.

Not Dick. Anyone who thinks the D stands for *dick* needs to get their mind out of the gutter.

I brace myself for the shenanigans that will surely ensue as the plane takes off, and as it lands and I stare out the window at the familiar landscape, it feels like home.

It's so strange how two places feel like home, but I spend more than half the year in Vegas, and I miss it when I'm gone. As much as I love Fallon Ridge, there's just something about Vegas that calls to me.

I spot the skyline made up of hotels starting from the south end of the strip—Mandalay Bay, Luxor, Excalibur, MGM, and so on down the road to the Cosmopolitan and the back of Planet Hollywood, Paris, Caesar's Palace, where the Big D Bash is set to be held starting tomorrow, and all the way north toward the Stratosphere.

There's just something magical about this city. It's not all roses all the time. While some dreams are born here, others die here. The excitement some feel turns into an addiction to others—addictions to gambling, or drugs, or alcohol, or women, or food. It can be overwhelming, but it can also be the greatest place in the world.

As we move slowly along toward the cut-off date for my potential extension, I can't help but hope with everything I have that the Aces sign me to another year. I want to stay here. I'd love a lengthy career playing for one team.

I have friends on other teams. Some are happy, while others aren't. There isn't much not to love about playing for the Vegas Aces, that's for damn sure.

I sign a few autographs and take a few selfies as I get off the plane, par for the course given I'm back in my hometown where I'm most recognized.

I shoot off a text to the Thursday Night Crew once I'm in an Uber toward Caesar's, where I managed to secure a suite.

Me: *What's the plan for tonight? Plane just got in and I'm on my way toward Caesar's.*

I get a hit back from Travis right away.

Travis: *Cory and me already out drinking.*

Me: *Where?*

Travis: *Not sure how the fuck you spell it, but that club at MGM.*

I chuckle quietly in the backseat. Hakkasan is notoriously the celebrity hangout in Vegas, so I assume he means that place.

Me: *I'll check in and drop my bag then meet you there.*

Travis: *We'll come to you. We were thinking a high-stakes room and some BJ.*
Me: *Blow jobs?*
Travis: *Blackjack, you dumb shit. Although now that you mention it…*
Cory: *Stop looking at me like that, Woods.*

I chuckle again to myself.

Me: *I'll meet you in the high stakes area in an hour. For blackjack.*
Travis: *For blackjack.*
Patrick: *Will you dumbfucks shut up?*
Austin: *I'm finishing an appearance but I'll swing by after.*

Jaxon and Deon are still out of town, but it looks like there will be four of us ready to take Caesar's for all it's worth.

I check in, stop in my room, and call Tessa to let her know I've arrived.

"Hey," she answers softly.

"I miss you already." I move toward the window to check out my view. My suite looks out over the Bellagio fountains, and they happen to be going off as I gaze down. It's relaxing, and all I can think is how I wish Tessa was here with me.

"I miss you, too."

"I just called to let you know I'm here at my hotel. I'm looking down at the Bellagio fountains right now from my room," I say.

She hums softly. "Sounds amazing. Send me a picture."

"As soon as we hang up, I will." I perch on the edge of the chair next to the window to enjoy the view. "Have I missed anything since I've been gone?"

She chuckles softly. "It hasn't even been half a day yet. And no. The answer is a solid nope. How's the hamstring?"

"I barely feel it at all since you worked your magic. How about you? Any bleeding?"

"None today," she says.

"Thank God," we murmur at the same time.

"Do you have plans for tonight?" she asks.

"I'm meeting my buddies for some blackjack in a bit, but other than that, nothing special." I think about how most twenty-five-year-old dudes would take this town by storm, and I feel suddenly a little lame.

She clears her throat. "What do you think the party will be like tomorrow?"

"Lots of people in swimsuits, live music, and plenty of alcohol," I say. "Ben usually throws an end of summer bash with all the same elements, but I think he's doing this one instead this year. He's got two babies he wants to get back to, so I think the party guy of the league has actually settled down."

"Shocking everyone," she says, and we both laugh. "Someone else will have to fill those big shoes."

"Maybe Travis," I suggest.

We stay on the line a little longer, and by the time I head down, I spot my buddies already gathering near the high stakes area with drinks in hand. I'm the last to arrive, and my hand is empty. On that note, I take a detour at the bar, grab a beer, then head toward the guys, who are waiting for me.

And that's all it takes.

A three-minute detour to grab a beer causes chaos.

We're swarmed, the four of us. Three wide receivers and one tight end in their hometown hanging at a popular Vegas casino for the night…I suppose we should've seen it coming.

It's mostly women, and from the looks of it, it's two or three bachelorette parties filled with women clamoring for the attention of a professional athlete. What a story to go home with, right?

What happens in Vegas stays in Vegas…unless you fuck a celebrity. That goes home with bragging rights.

Drunk bachelorettes are catnip for my boys. Cory's cheesing it up big time for every selfie request, two girls are hanging off Austin—one grasping onto each bicep, Travis is already making out with some girl he'll never see again, and then there's me…the guy getting annoyed because these gorgeous women keep bumping into my arm and causing me to spill my beer.

I'm just not the party guy my buddies want me to be. I'd rather be at home watching the next episode of *Outlander* with my pregnant girlfriend.

I suck in a breath then chug my beer.

It's going to be a long night.

Hell, it's going to be a long *weekend*.

CHAPTER 30

Tessa

I shouldn't be stewing over the photos I keep seeing him tagged in, but I'm stewing.

It's only Thursday night. He's only been gone for a few hours, really. And yet a new picture pops up every few minutes. He looks like he's having the time of his life. Last I heard, he was meeting his friends for some blackjack. Instead, it looks like he's the entertainment at a bachelorette party.

And I'm only guessing that because in one of the photos where he's tagged, a girl wearing a headband with plastic penises swaying in the breeze is kissing him on the cheek.

Rage blossoms in my chest.

I'm not mad that he went. I can't be mad he went—not when I practically forced him to go. He should celebrate. He should see his friends. He deserves that.

But these girls showering him with attention…that's not really so much my cup of tea.

I trust him.

I remind myself of that over and over.

I trust him.

I do. He wouldn't cheat on me. He loves me. He bought me a damn house, for crying out loud.

But still…history keeps knocking on my thoughts.

My little encounter with Cam's wife in the bathroom at the Christmas party still plays in my mind. Was she just marking her territory when she warned me to keep my hands to myself? Or was there something deeper there, some fear or knowledge that he was cheating on her?

And my mother…she didn't seem surprised that my dad had a million other children running around—at least not the same way I was surprised.

The men in my life were cheaters. That doesn't mean Tristan is, but he's got an awful lot of temptation for one night of fun right there in front of him while the pregnant girl he pledged forever to is four states and over fifteen hundred miles away.

And it's not just the pictures with the women, though those are plenty. It's other photographs, too. Tristan with Cory, or Austin, or Travis—or some combination of the four of them. His head's thrown back in laughter in one. It's a little different from how I pictured his night going with the whole *I'm meeting my buddies for some blackjack in a bit, but other than that, nothing special* line.

I close Instagram rather than continuing to do this to myself.

I'm tired anyway, and all it's doing is reminding me that he already has a life.

He lives in Las Vegas. He has a circle of friends. He has a career, and he has a *place* there.

He keeps telling me he wants me, wants the baby, wants *us*…and I believe him. But it's hard to reconcile those words with the pictures I'm seeing. Women will always want pictures with him. They'll always stop and ask for a selfie with one of the best-looking guys in the NFL. Journalists or paparazzi will always be tailing him for the latest gossip.

How do I fit into that?

How does this baby fit into that?

I don't want the spotlight—not for her, and not for myself. But it's inevitable because a spotlight shines brightly on Tristan Higgins wherever he goes.

My phone starts ringing, and it's a number I don't recognize.

I should just go to bed.

I should ignore it.

But something drives me to answer it.

And when I do, I wish I never had.

"Hello?"

"Tessa, hi. It's Savannah…Tristan's ex-wife."

"How did you get my number?" I demand, my hackles rising as I suddenly wish he was here—or, at the very least, that he was next door right now rather than halfway across the country.

"Does it matter?" she asks. "Look, I have things I need to tell you. Things you don't know about the man you've brainwashed."

"Excuse me?" I say, and I sit up as I rest a protective hand over my stomach.

Jeez, I really don't need this stress right now.

"I haven't brainwashed him," I protest.

"Right," she says. "Says every minister's daughter ever."

I can picture her rolling her eyes.

Hang up, Tessa. Hang up.

"What do you want?" I ask as I ignore my very intelligent inner voice.

I try to clear my head. I should record this conversation as evidence against her, but I don't even know if that's possible to do on a phone. I glance around for a tablet, or my laptop—but everything's in the kitchen plugged in and charging.

"Did you know that after you *disappeared*, sweet Tristan had a, well, *tryst* with none other than Miss Tiffany Gable?" she asks.

"What?" I gasp. How would she know that?

And why is she telling me?

"I know!" she says, her voice dramatically sarcastic. "I was shocked, too. I thought he was so heartbroken over you that he'd be celibate forever when you left to go have his baby unbeknownst to him. But trust me…he broke that vow long before he met me. Then he broke it with me more than a time or two if you know what I mean."

My chest tightens at the mention of our history and the things he doesn't know about, and my stomach twists at the thought of him being intimate with her.

Was he the same way with her as he is with me?

I shake off the thought.

I don't know who this woman thinks she is…but I do know she's extremely dangerous. "Why are you telling me this?"

"You should know everything about the man you want to spend forever with, my sweet darling girl," she says, and the sugar in her voice is enough to give me a toothache. "He's back here in Vegas right now probably about to bring one of those bachelorettes back up to his suite while you're back home growing Cam Foster's baby. Ugh, it's all just so…what's the word? Oh, that's right—it's all so *cliché*."

Cam Foster.

Oh my God.

I thought she was just bluffing.

She knows the truth about the baby.

Both babies.

I draw in a shaky breath as I try to figure out what to say next. I don't have to say anything, though, because she keeps dumping more and more onto my lap.

Honest **MISTAKE**

"Anyway, Tiff and I are great friends now after your little craft thingie, and she filled me in on *all* the deets about what happened after you just took off on poor Tris. I guess he got epically hammered one night, and Tiff swooped in and, well, I probably don't need to tell you the rest, but let's just say Mr. Higgins must have some mighty strong swimmers in there because there was this whole pregnancy scare—can you imagine? You're off having his baby while he's screwing Fallon's favorite Gable. And I myself had a pregnancy scare, so potentially he could've had kids with three different baby mamas! Or even more, who knows?" She rambles on as my chest grows tighter and tighter, as that knot in my stomach twists more and more, as my head buzzes louder and louder.

Is this true?

Did Tristan sleep with Tiffany?

I shouldn't care what he did after I left. It doesn't really matter, and I can't sit here and get mad about secrets he's keeping from me when I'm keeping secrets of my own.

But if it's true, it's a sting that hurts pretty damn bad.

"I'm hanging up now," I hiss.

She cackles. "Oh, no you aren't sweetie."

"What do you want?"

"If you want me to keep what I know about your history a secret from our beloved Tristan, then you need to break it off with him," she demands.

And there it is.

The blackmail.

The part I wish I'd been able to record.

Break it off with him?

Not a chance in hell.

I'm too scared to say that, though, so I simply end the call. My fingers tremble as I hit the red button, but I don't know what else to do. I click off my phone and toss it away from me onto my bed.

It starts ringing again. I know it's her, but I refuse to answer.

I also know she's not the type of woman who will be ignored.

She was blackmailing Tristan, and he was brave enough to admit the truth to his coach so she could get him to back down.

I need to be brave enough to tell Tristan the truth before she does.

Just like he was brave enough to tell me about him and Tiffany.

CHAPTER 31

Tessa

I toss and turn all night.

Well, tossing and turning is generous. It's more like I readjust and hump my big-ass pregnancy pillow as I try to quiet my mind and find some sort of comfortable position to sleep in that doesn't make my hips burn.

That's becoming a harder and harder task as time goes on, but it's the quieting my mind thing I'm having real trouble with.

I can't stop replaying my conversation with Savannah, and I hate that I don't even know where she is. She indicated that she's in Vegas—I think she said something about how Tristan is *here* now, but that could be my memory playing tricks on me.

But that means she might be closer to him, and I don't know what I did by hanging up on her. I'm not sure if I provoked an already angry bear or if she'll simply let it go.

Of course she won't let it go. It's Tristan she's fighting for, and if there's anybody on Earth worth fighting for, it's that man.

I have a doctor appointment this morning, and my mom volunteered to go with me since Tristan's out of town. After breakfast, we head toward Davenport.

"The ultrasound looks good," the doctor tells me. "I'd like you to stay on pelvic rest the next couple weeks, but you can resume normal activity otherwise."

As soon as I hear that, I think about surprising Tristan in Vegas. "So it's fine to travel?" I ask.

My mom's eyes edge over to me as she gives me a disapproving look.

"Perfectly safe, though international travel isn't recommended after twenty-eight weeks," she says. "If you're staying in the US, usually it's thirty-six weeks provided it's not a high-risk pregnancy."

"Am I considered at risk?"

She shakes her head. "A low-lying placenta itself isn't considered a high-risk condition, but do take it easy. It's safest to travel in the second trimester, and you're at the start of your third right now."

Perfect.

It's safe to fly to Tristan.

As soon as I get home, I'm booking my ticket.

My mom tries to talk me out of it on the way home. "He'll be back Monday morning," she argues. "Let him have his boy's weekend. Maybe he'll do this in lieu of a bachelor party. Have you picked a date yet?"

I shake my head. "I think I want to wait until the baby's here. Maybe next year sometime. I'm not in a rush, and he just got divorced." I think of Savannah's blackmail. I think of Tiffany Gable and all the other women who want him for themselves. I even think of Stephanie and how she wants to come between Tristan and me.

Maybe rushing the wedding is the best thing we can do. We both know it's what we want. We both know it's inevitable—that *we* are inevitable. It might not completely stop the Savannahs from blackmailing or the Tiffanys from clamoring after my man or the Stephanies from working to break us apart, but it would strengthen our bond and, in turn, our fight against them.

What if I fly to Vegas this afternoon and we come back to Fallon Ridge *married* on Monday morning?

My mother would kill me if she missed my wedding…but she missed a lot of things in my life, and we're still okay. She'd get over it, and we'd surely plan another wedding for public consumption.

The more I think about it, the more I love the idea.

The plan continues to formulate in my mind as I navigate toward home. I run to the bathroom, of course, once I get home, but when I'm done, my mom meets me in the kitchen. "I need to head over to the church a while. You'll be okay?"

I nod.

"You're not jetting off to Vegas, are you?"

I sigh. "Of course I am, Mama."

She laughs. "Just be safe, okay?" She presses a kiss to my cheek and a hand to my belly. "Both of you."

"We will."

She heads out the door, and I get myself a cup of ice water as I start searching flights to Vegas. I'm debating whether to text him first or to surprise him by just showing up.

Texting first would ruin the surprise, obviously, but it would show him how much I trust him. I'm not just showing up out of the blue like I'm trying to catch him in the act of something.

On the other hand, a surprise sounds like fun.

I decide to settle for something in the middle.

Me: *Doctor appointment went well today. She cleared me for normal activity (but, sadly, still on pelvic rest).*

I wait a while for a reply, but one doesn't come through.

And that's when my brain starts playing tricks on me.

He's not writing back because he's at a pool and doesn't have his phone in his pocket. That's the first thing I tell myself. But when an hour passes and he still hasn't responded, I start to get annoyed. It's probably the damn pregnancy hormones, but I can't help it. Annoyance turns fairly quickly to accusations as they play out in my brain.

In my head, he's in his swim trunks in a hot tub in Vegas surrounded by a bevy of gorgeous, scantily clad women as they feed him grapes and kiss him and tip whiskey onto his tongue since his hands are otherwise occupied under the water.

I send another text with that image in my mind even though a smarter version of myself would definitely not.

Me: *I'm sure you're busy with all the gorgeous women of Vegas so I won't bother booking a flight out to surprise you.*

I shouldn't have sent that one. I immediately regret it.

I'm about to type a retraction text when the doorbell rings.

I'm not expecting any visitors, and my mom's at work, so my first assumption is that it's Stephanie since her favorite thing to do is drop by unannounced.

When I open the door, I gasp.

It's not Stephanie.

It's Christine Foster.

Dr. Cameron Foster's wife.

Her eyes are hard and angry, and in her hand she holds a manila folder.

A sick feeling twists in my stomach and I feel a little dizzy. I have a feeling I already know what's in that envelope.

She must've found the papers Tristan's lawyer sent over to Cam.

She glances down at my stomach. "Cute baby bump. Is it my husband's? Because he has rights, you know."

She takes the manila folder between her hands and rips it in two, and my chest races. I grab onto the wall as the dizziness

Honest **MISTAKE**

intensifies, the whole room spinning around me for a second, and then everything goes black.

CHAPTER 32

Tristan

It seems like everyone made it back for this weekend. I've been making the rounds, catching up with people I haven't seen in months, and it's been refreshing.

It's the last weekend to raise hell before the voluntary veteran minicamp, which most of us will be attending anyway. What better place to raise hell than back in Vegas with your brothers?

I'm in the pool with Austin and Travis, and I glance around at the party happening all around me. Loud music comes from the deejay booth, but Ben tells us some local bands are coming by a little later. Some workers from the hotel are setting up a lunch buffet, and I'm currently working on pacing myself so I'm not drunk all day. There's a long way to go from now until midnight, when the party will pause for ten or so hours of sleep before resuming again tomorrow.

Ben Olson walks around in his flamingo swim trunks, the life of every party as he greets guests with a solo cup filled with beer permanently affixed to his palm. His girl comes and goes, and their twins are up in a suite with her mom and his dad when she's able to escape down for a while. He hangs with Cooper Noah, a retired baseball player, and he introduces me as his buddy. From what I gather, Cooper and Ben's wife work together, and they've gotten close.

Jack Dalton's here, too, in one of the cabanas as he sips whiskey. His wife, Kate, lies on a lounge chair like she hasn't had a second of peace in a while. She probably hasn't between her newborn and her stepson, JJ, plus the start of her career as she dives headfirst into owning her own interior design firm.

Ellie lies on the chair beside Kate. The table between them has two half-drunk margaritas on it, and both appear to be sleeping. They just came down an hour or so ago, and Luke told me their kids are all playing together in another suite with Elizabeth, their nanny. Another table with another partial margarita sits on Ellie's other side, and where Josh Nolan's wife Nicki is asleep on the lounge chair on the other side of it.

Luke pops in and out of his brother's cabana, but mostly he's in business mode as he talks with his clients and drums up more business for his agency and, in turn, his wife. Those two are quite the team, and I'm honored to be friends with them.

I can't wait for Tessa to start her job with Ellie, too. She's going to love it.

I can't believe how it's all working out.

I wish I could call her, or at least text her, but this morning when I left the room, I decided to leave my phone. I can't use it in the water, and I didn't particularly want to have to track it all day. We talked last night, and we'll talk again tonight, and soon I'll be back home so life can resume right where we left off.

I glance around and spot Brandon Fletcher, who was our star quarterback before we acquired Jack Dalton and is now relegated to the back-up QB. He's chatting up some ladies with a group of my buddies including Jaxon and Damon.

Cory and Patrick are by the bar with Deon Miller and a couple defenders, Richard Garrett and Dave Redmayne, are behind them with their wives. I see Cason, the other final wide receiver on the Aces roster, talking with a couple guys from the practice squad—Andrew Miles, Jonathan Winters, Sean Banks.

I can't help but wonder whether all six of the wide receivers from last year will play a full season together again this year. It's rare for every rostered player in a position to return year after year, but those men—Travis Woods, Cory Marshall, Damon Green, Cason Swanson, and Josh Nolan—are like family to me, and I can't imagine an Aces season where all six of us aren't training, practicing, and playing together.

There's been enough chaos, upheaval, and change in my life. I'm ready for the next phase where I can focus on the three big Fs: family, football, and the future…and where I can start making dad jokes, obviously.

I get out of the water and head to the bar for another beer when Cory walks over with his phone. "I need to show you something," he says. He clicks open JustFans, a subscription app where creators can sell original content…also known as the latest and greatest way to see hot girls naked.

I roll my eyes. "Dude, I've got a girl. I don't need your porn site to see titties."

I expect him to laugh, too, but his brows are furrowed together as he pulls something up on the app. He hands me his phone, and ice seems to grip onto my chest as I look at what he's showing me.

Tessa Taylor, age 25, Chicago, Illinois. Engaged to NFL wide receiver.

And above the short bio is her picture.

Her picture.

My Tessa.

"Dude, isn't that your girl?" Cory asks somewhere in my periphery.

I click on the content tab and find some video hooks. I click the first one, and I spot a woman's figure shown from the neck down. Her head is off the screen, but her tits sure aren't. She's naked, and she's dancing—if you can call it that. It's gyrating, really, and she's not subtle.

But she's also not Tessa.

The video clip ends and a big bar comes across the screen asking me to pay just nineteen-ninety-nine for another five minutes of this shit.

I blow out a breath.

Someone's impersonating Tessa on what's essentially a pornographic website, and I'm going to figure out who…and why.

I hand Cory his phone and bust my ass upstairs to get my phone.

I see the last text she sent.

Tessa: *I'm sure you're busy with all the gorgeous women of Vegas so I won't bother booking a flight out to surprise you.*

What the fuck?

I don't bother texting back, opting instead to call.

But the call goes directly to voicemail.

Maybe she had to turn her phone off because she booked a ticket to come see me after all.

That's my hope, anyway.

"Hey," I say. "I need to talk to you. Where are you? I'm so glad you're cleared to travel. Yes, come out here. Or I'll come back there. I need to see you. Call me back."

I hang up and realize my mistake immediately. I gave her two options on the call—she could come here, or I could go there, and now I'm stuck waiting here to see if she chose the first option.

Fuck it. I slide my phone into my swim trunks. I'm not missing her again.

CHAPTER 33

Tristan

I called her a little before noon, just before the lunch buffet. When it's six and I still haven't heard from her, I start to get worried.

If she turned off her phone to fly to Vegas, she'd be here by now.

I've tried texting her a handful of times, but she's not responding. In fact, the messages aren't even showing as delivered.

The first band takes the stage, some local group I've never heard of, and they're decent but I can't get into the sounds. Instead, I'm checking my phone every four seconds.

Another band plays, and we drink, and another band.

I glance at the clock. It's almost ten here, which means it's almost midnight in Iowa. Too late to call her mom to check on her.

But maybe not too late to call *my* parents.

They go to bed early, but I'd classify this as an emergency. I don't know who else to call, anyway, and so I settle on my mother. I head inside the hotel and pace the small lobby near the exit toward the pool.

My mom picks up on the first ring. "Tristan, is everything okay?" She sounds panicked, but of course she would be. I don't usually call her at midnight.

"Sorry to bother you," I say, not answering her question about whether everything's okay because *I don't know* if everything's okay. "Have you seen Tessa today? She isn't answering her phone and I'm worried."

She clears her throat sleepily, and I hear her bed squeak as she likely gets out of it. "I haven't seen her, honey. Hang on, I'm checking to see if her car is in the driveway."

I wait as nerves rattle my chest.

"It's not there. Have you tried her mom?" she asks.

"No. I didn't want to wake her."

"I'm sure if something was wrong, Janet would've reached out to you," she says, trying her best to calm my nerves.

"Yeah, you're probably right." I lean against the wall as the edges of a headache start to creep in.

"Get some rest, honey. I'm sure she'll call you first thing in the morning," she says.

"Thanks for checking, Mom. Goodnight," I murmur.

"Night, honey. Love you."

She hangs up, and I just head up to my room. I know Ben has big ticket names on the marquee for tonight, but I feel less like partying out there and more like either heading to Coax. Not for the third floor, obviously. Just to hang out, play pool, and get away from the spotlight for a while.

Visiting Coax might feel like I'm betraying Tessa, though. I'm not going for the sex floor, but that's hardly a defense since it still exists there.

I haven't mentioned the club to her, mostly because I'm not sure it merits mentioning and because I signed that NDA. I haven't purposely kept it from her, either.

Still, it's calling to me.

I push away the temptation to go, and I go upstairs instead.

I raid the minibar and drink myself stupid. That's when the real bad decisions begin.

I head back downstairs and find Travis.

"Coax?" I suggest low in his ear over the loud music from the band on stage. They're good, and I move to the beat a little as I listen.

His brows furrow as he looks at me. "*Coax*?" he repeats in a low voice. "You're engaged, and your girl who isn't here is having a baby, and you want to go to *Coax* right now?"

"Just to play pool and have a drink." I shrug. "She's not answering my calls, and her last text was all accusatory. Might as well do something worthy of those accusations, right?"

"You're drunk," he says flatly. "They won't let you in drunk."

Dammit. He's right.

"Fuck," I mutter. It's just as well, though my alcohol-muddled brain doesn't want to admit it.

Some girl I've never seen before is dancing next to me in only a bikini, and she bumps into me on accident. She turns toward me to apologize, and she has that same glazed look in her eyes that I do.

"Oh my God, it's Tristan Higgins!" she squeals. She throws her arms around my neck. "Congratulations on the divorce. Care to celebrate in private?"

I chuckle. "Thanks for the offer." I allow my eyes to flick down to her chest. "You're hot as fuck, but I'm not single."

She doesn't seem to care, and she doesn't bother untangling herself. "Someone made quick work of that. Wish it was me."

I squeeze her a little in a hug. "She's the love of my life. The woman I always should've been with."

"Lucky her," she says.

I'm the lucky one. I should say it, should proclaim it to everyone, but suddenly I'm exhausted. I shouldn't have come back down here. It was a bad choice, and except for the horrible decision that was Savannah, I'm generally not known for making bad decisions…unless I'm as far gone as I am right now.

The last time I was quite this wasted, the whole Tiffany Gable thing happened. I thought she was Tessa. I don't even remember having sex with her. I don't know how my dick could have possibly worked that night, and I'm certain I was moaning Tessa's name the entire time.

Tiffany took advantage of my situation, and then I almost had to deal with the consequences that would have tied me to her for life when we had a pregnancy scare.

I push the thought away. Thinking about that time in my life only makes me feel sick. I bid the girl still hugging me goodnight, and then I head upstairs.

Except I'm stopped in my tracks on the way up.

"Tristan?" a familiar voice calls out to me.

I turn to look at the woman, and she rushes into my arms for a hug.

It takes me a second to recognize her. I've seen every square inch of her naked flesh, yet seeing her outside of Coax is…confusing.

"Brandi," I murmur into her hair. "What are you doing here?"

"When I saw this party was for you, I had to come see you. Congratulations on the divorce. I didn't even know you were married." She lifts a shoulder and tilts her head. "It explains a lot."

I can't help the grunt of a chuckle. It explains nothing, actually, but I don't have a chance to tell her that because she fires off her next question.

"How come you haven't been around lately?"

I shrug. "Been busy."

"And this girl I keep seeing you with online? Is she the wife?"

I shake my head. "No. She's the future wife, not the *ex*-wife."

Her brows arch. "You're already engaged?"

I nod.

"Wow. I didn't even get a chance to slip in there."

I don't bother telling her it wouldn't have mattered. It's inaccurate to say she had her shot because she didn't. Not really. I never found myself interested in her, and maybe it's because I'm not the type of guy who goes to a place like that to pick up women.

The thought of bringing Tessa up to the third floor someday occurs to me. Sliding my hand up her thigh, making her squirm as we watch the things in front of us we're not supposed to see.

I shake the thought out of my head. I still can't imagine even *telling* her that I went there. The fact that I never had sex in it wouldn't matter.

It's a dark thought to have when I'm drunk, but it's not even that she wouldn't understand. Maybe she would, maybe she wouldn't, though I'd lean toward the latter.

It has more to do with the thought that I'm ashamed.

Every time I stepped onto the third floor, I felt weird about being there. It always felt wrong.

And now, seeing Brandi out of context, those feelings of shame rush back over me.

It's in the past.

My membership may be good for another six or seven months, but I don't know if I see myself going back there again, and certainly not to the third floor.

"Well, it was nice seeing you," I say awkwardly, and then I give her a quick hug and beeline the hell out of there.

When I get back to my room, I promptly pass out.

Drinking myself stupid wasn't my best choice.

I wake up with a worse headache than I had when I went to bed, and no amount of greasy eggs and bacon is going to help.

I check my phone, and I still haven't heard from her. I try calling. No answer.

I finally decide to call her mom.

It's Saturday morning, though, so of course she doesn't answer. She's probably busy at the church ahead of tomorrow's services.

I try texting Tessa one more time before I head down toward the pool.

Very few people are around just yet, but Ben Olson is down there with his wife Kaylee, and he looks awfully chipper for someone who drank beer the entire day yesterday.

"It's our guest of honor!" he yells when he sees me.

"Can you turn the volume down?" I whine, and he laughs as he musses up my hair.

"Hangover?" he correctly guesses, and I wince and nod. "Jack Dalton taught me his special hangover cure. I can't tell you what's in it, and it tastes like the back of a donkey's balls, but it works."

"How do you know what the back of donkey balls taste like?" I ask.

He laughs. "Go get a plate full of the breakfast buffet, and I'll whip up the concoction for you. Meet me in Cabana Two."

I nod and head over toward the buffet. Today's not the day I start eating right to get back into season shape. I've got plenty of time for that, and minicamp can be the start of it. I fill my plate with scrambled eggs, opting for the super runny ones even though they're gross, sausage, bacon, and pancakes. I grab another plate and fill it with fruit to try to restore some vitamins and hydration, and then I head over to the cabana.

Ben's in there stirring a pitcher. "I made a whole pitcher because I'm guessing you won't be alone," he declares proudly, and I can't help a laugh. He pours me a pint glass full of what looks like a pretty disgusting concoction, and I wrinkle my nose as he hands it over.

I take a sip, and yep…it's vile. Then I suck it up and chug the whole glass.

My mouth burns a little. "Why is my mouth burning? What the fuck did you just poison me with?"

He laughs. "That would be the dash of cayenne pepper. I *might* have put in more than a dash. Then there's lemon, honey, sprite, and coconut water mixed with a mystery ingredient," he says. He holds up his hands. "That's as much as I can reveal."

"Well, you were right. That's exactly how I'd imagine the back of donkey balls to taste."

"You're welcome," Ben says gallantly.

"I'm glad you're down here. I, uh…I think I need to head back home. I can't get in touch with my fiancée. I think something might be wrong."

His brows furrow and he nods. "Of course. Go. I understand completely."

"I don't want to miss the party," I say.

He laughs and shakes his head. "I sprung it on you last-minute because they had an opening. Some things in life are more important than a party, and nobody learned that faster than me." He glances over at his wife. "It doesn't mean the party's over, man. It just means you've got a partner to party with."

I give him a sad smile. "I need to go find my partner."

"Go. Good luck. Let me know how it all turns out."

I nod and run up to my room. A flight leaves in about an hour, so I book it and race to the airport, boarding just in time.

The flight home drags. I'm nervous and I'm exhausted but at least I'm not hungover thanks to Ben's miracle donkey ball concoction.

I spent my time staring out the window willing everything to be okay, but the more I will it, the more sure I become that something is very, very wrong.

Not hearing from her for the last twenty-four hours tells me just how much her disappearance the first time still affects me.

It left a scar that still burns even after all this time.

It left me with a heinous fear of abandonment, and maybe I'm just being dramatic, or maybe it's a real psychological issue that will never heal. Maybe I'll always be scared she'll just disappear again, leaving me with nothing like she did the first time.

I don't know if I can come back from that for a second time. Not when everything felt so perfect. So right. Not when our future together was just within my grasp.

We finally land in Chicago, but then it's nearly another three hours toward Fallon Ridge. With the time difference from Vegas, it's after six o'clock by the time I get into town.

My chest tightens when I see the big house on the corner. *Our house.*

We should be moving in this week. Most of our furniture is scheduled to be delivered tomorrow.

My heart thunders in my chest as I turn down Hickory Tree Lane, and as I loop around onto Oak Tree Lane, I can see it from here.

Her car is still missing from her mother's driveway.

I park in front of my parents' house, and I jump out of my truck, rushing to the Taylors' front door. I ring the bell, and

Honest MISTAKE

Tessa's mom glances out the window a moment later. When she sees me, her brows furrow.

"Hi, honey," she greets me as she opens the door.

"Hi, Mrs. Taylor," I whisper.

"It's Mil now, remember?"

I can't seem to muster a laugh of any sort, and she gazes at me with concern.

"What are you doing back? What's wrong?" she asks.

"Where is she?" My voice suddenly won't work, and my words come out in a strangled whisper.

"She took off for Chicago," she says, and her words bring me back seven years ago when her dad said nearly the exact same thing to me.

Only she never returned.

His words were followed by, "She told me to break it off with you before she left."

My knees nearly give out as I wait for her mom to say the same thing to me.

Devastation rolls through me as that same feeling of abandonment stabs into my stomach. Her last text to me runs through my mind again. She was upset, mad at me, sure I was cheating on her. But of course her mind would go there after what happened with Cam and her father. She has to know I'm not like the others.

I have to tell her.

But she won't answer me.

I grip onto the wooden doorframe as I try to hold myself up. She's gone again—and to the same place, no less.

History can't be repeating itself. Not after everything we've been through.

Can it?

To be continued in book 4, NO MISTAKE.

ACKNOWLEDGMENTS

I'll save my acknowledgments for the final book since I know you're ready to get to *No Mistake*… and I can't wait for you to see what's next.

xoxo,
Lisa Suzanne

ABOUT THE AUTHOR

Lisa Suzanne is a romance author who resides in Arizona with her husband and two kids. She's a former high school English teacher and college composition instructor. When she's not cuddling or chasing her kids, she can be found working on her latest book or watching reruns of *Friends*.

ALSO BY LISA SUZANNE

HOME GAME
Vegas Aces Book One
#1 Bestselling Sports Romance

A LITTLE LIKE DESTINY
A Little Like Destiny Book One
#1 Bestselling Rock Star Romance

Printed in Great Britain
by Amazon